CW00485912

# Forbidden Candy

ZANE MENZY

Copyright © 2019 Zane Menzy

All rights reserved.

# DEDICATION

Coffee and nicotine. I'm your biggest fan.

# FORBIDDEN CANDY

## CANDY BOY BOOK NO. 3

# CHAPTER 1

*Did I go too far?*

Dwight asked himself this question repeatedly as he sped down the street, trying to put as much distance between himself and the scene of twisted vengeance he'd just dished out. What he'd just done was probably the cruellest thing in his whole life—and that was saying something for a man with sadistic tastes. Tying Levi up and blindfolding him with his stepfather's stinky underwear then letting a stranger inside to have sex with him before walking out and leaving Levi there was a whole new level of cruel.

Dwight had always prided himself on being a man of principle, a man of conviction. Sure, those principles sometimes fell victim to life's shades of grey but he was still someone who owned his actions and held himself responsible for their outcomes. And that's what he was forcing Levi to do; be held responsible for his actions.

*Don't feel guilty. He fucking deserved it for what he planned to do to you.*

Dwight's inner voice made him feel better. Levi did deserve it. The spoilt brat had lured him upstairs to his bedroom under false pretences, telling Dwight he was keen to fool around again but all the while planning on videoing the whole thing. Dwight shuddered as he thought about his lucky escape. Had he not gone snooping inside the house while Levi mowed the lawns then he would have never found the hidden camera and the little shit would have had him by the balls. Dwight knew without a shadow of a doubt Levi would have used that video to blackmail him into doing things he never wanted to do. Submissive things. Degrading things. Things like he had just done to Levi.

"Nobody fucks me," he muttered to himself. Dwight sensed that Levi probably thought the same thing about himself not so long ago; that he would never bite the pillow and never let another man inside him. Dwight had read the Candy Boy blog long enough to know that Levi was dominant at heart but twice within a week the hazel-eyed hunk had given his arse up. Three times if you count Blondie's guest appearance.

Dwight cringed as he recalled watching his young blond pal fuck Levi's arse raw. Blondie was no porn star that's for sure. The kid lost his lollies almost immediately, giving away his lack of experience and how much he must have liked the sight and feel of a naked, writhing Levi beneath him. Dwight couldn't argue with that. Levi was unbelievably attractive—even with a pair of stinky briefs covering his face.

While Blondie failed to fuck like a real man, he did at least ejaculate like one, filling Levi with an abundance of cum. Dwight had felt it when he pressed the tip of his finger inside Levi's ravaged hole, feeling a plentiful amount of young ball juice. This final knife to Levi's pride was cold and calculated and it served a selfish purpose. Before Blondie had fucked Levi bare, Dwight may have felt like he owned Levi but that had done little to battle the inconvenient feelings he had for his son's best friend. Not now though. Levi Candy was nothing more than damaged goods, another man's sloppy seconds, and Dwight Stephenson didn't pine for sloppy seconds.

Keeping one hand on the steering wheel, he patted his shorts pocket that had the tiny camera in it. A dark smile spread across his lips as he thought about watching the video when he got home. He only wished he could have caught on tape the look on Levi's face when he saw who it was Dwight had text to come untie him.

*That'll fucking learn ya for messing with me and my boy.*

The sound of his phone buzzing with a phone call made him pull over. A glance at the screen told him it was Blondie. Dwight answered the call, annoyed by the young guy's impatience to talk already. "Whatcha want, Blondie?"

"What did you just drag me into?"

"What do you mean?" Dwight replied, playing dumb.

"You told me you had someone keen for a kinky hook up but something tells me that wasn't the case."

*No shit, Sherlock.*

Dwight took a deep breath. "Just take my word for it when I tell you that maggot had it coming."

"Then why did it feel like it was—"

"Karma," Dwight said, cutting the boy off. "That's all it was. Karma. So stop ya worrying."

"I'm not worried," Blondie said calmly. "I'm just curious. Why would you trick someone like that?"

"He needed to be taught a lesson. End of."

"That's a pretty intense lesson." Blondie exhaled heavily. "What did he do wrong?"

"That's between me and him."

"Surely I'm entitled to know something about it considering what you just made me do."

Dwight coughed out a humourless laugh. "Don't make it sound like I put a gun to ya head. I could tell by the look in your eyes you wanted to fuck him. Shit, you barely lasted thirty seconds you were that keen."

"Shut up," Blondie said defensively.

"I'm just teasing ya." Dwight chuckled. "But you might want to consider coming to visit me sometime so I can teach you how to fuck."

"You reckon?" Blondie's voice had a smile in it.

"Yep. If you spent a whole weekend with me then you'd learn a thing or two. You might not be able to walk properly afterwards but you'd at least know how to fuck like a pro."

Blondie laughed. "I told you, bro, I ain't really a bottom."

"I'm not your bro... *bro*." Dwight rolled his eyes. It wasn't that he hated being called that word he just hated hearing Blondie say it. Each time Blondie said the word it felt out of place. The boy wasn't effeminate but he was pushing his luck thinking he could throw that word around like the men who used it so easily. "Tuesday night at the tavern tells me otherwise."

"That was a one-off. You just caught me at the right moment."

"If you say so."

After a slight pause, Blondie gave his desperation away when he said in a flirty voice, "It's Friday today so maybe I could come to your place tonight and stay for the weekend and get some of this private tuition you're offering."

"Sorry, no can do," Dwight said bluntly.

"Oh," Blondie mumbled. "How come?"

"I'm busy."

"Are you sure?"

"I am sure," Dwight said bluntly.

"Maybe I should just go back and keep practicing on *Levi* until you get back," Blondie said spitefully.

Dwight nearly dropped his phone from shock. "Do you know him?"

"Yeah. Everyone in town knows Levi Candy."

Dwight shook his head, snapping out of his shock. "Why didn't you bloody tell me that you knew him?"

"I'm telling you now, aren't I?"

"You know what I mean. Why didn't you tell me when I let you in the house?"

"You told me I wasn't allowed to speak."

Dwight slapped a palm over his face, groaning. That was true. He had made it clear when he'd text Blondie that he was to turn up at 33 Shelter Grove immediately and not say a word the moment he stepped inside the house; just walk upstairs, get naked, and fuck the horny slut keen for a load. "How well do you know him?" he finally asked.

"Not hugely well but I've always had a thing for him even though he's an arrogant prick."

"He's certainly that," Dwight agreed.

"I always assumed he was straight. Apparently not." Blondie sniggered. "It's fucking hilarious knowing he has a daddy kink."

"Yep, hilarious," Dwight muttered. "Anyway, Blondie, I hope you were joking about going back to see him."

"Yeah, bro. It was just a joke."

"Good. I want you to forget about what happened today and pretend you were never there. Got it?"

"Got it. My lips are sealed," Blondie said.

"They bloody better be. I would never have invited you there if I had known you knew each other."

"I'm glad you invited me. Like I said, Levi's an arrogant prick and it feels awesome knowing I just fucked Fitzroy's king of the scene." Blondie laughed.

5

"Laugh all you like as long as it's to yourself."

"Chill, bro. I'm not even out so it's not like I am gonna go running around telling everyone."

"You're not out?"

"Nope. I've got a girlfriend."

"I see." Dwight should have felt sorry for the girlfriend dating a guy stupid enough to bareback other men behind her back but Blondie's hetero-facade suited Dwight just fine. As long as the kid was in the closet then there was less chance of him doing something stupid like saying something to Levi.

"Yeah me and Rachel have been together for—"

"I don't even know your name, Blondie, so what makes you think I wanna know the name of some bitch you're dating."

Blondie snorted. "Do you even know how rude you sound?"

"Not really. That would require giving a shit."

"I should probably hang up on you right now but you even sound sexy when you're being a cunt." When Dwight didn't respond, Blondie added in a pathetic little voice, "Are you sure you don't have time tonight to meet up? Even just for a quickie?"

"I just watched you empty your balls less than twenty minutes ago."

"I know but you know what they say, 'Young, dumb and full of cum.'"

It was the dumb part Dwight was worried about.

"I'll let you top me again," Blondie whispered, sounding like he was offering up the holy grail.

"I thought you just said last time was a one-off?"

"Yeah, well… maybe it's a twice-off?"

Dwight smiled. It was pathetically obvious this kid had it bad. One decent dicking and he was gagging for more. If Blondie's arse hadn't strangled his dick so much the night Dwight fucked him at the tavern then he would have assumed he'd found himself a hungry bottom in denial. But Blondie wasn't a hungry bottom. No, siree. He was a cocky little shit who was less-experienced than he claimed to be; his youth placing him in that dangerous place of vulnerability where you develop feelings for someone after just one fuck if they were hot enough. And Dwight knew he was hot enough.

"Come on," Blondie said. "I know how much you enjoyed drilling me last time."

"Did I?"

"You did," Blondie said before quietly adding, "Didn't you?"

"No, I did," Dwight said quickly.

"You know I'm better than Levi," Blondie said, trying his best to dress his jealousy up as bravado.

"You reckon?" Dwight scratched his neck, wondering if he could be bothered throwing this kid a bone by boning him before he left town.

"I'm not some sloppy faggot who calls guys Daddy." Blondie sniggered, probably thinking he was saying what Dwight wanted to hear.

The callousness of Blondie's snigger stirred something in Dwight. He felt offended on Levi's behalf. Obviously that was fucked-up considering how he'd just spent the afternoon on a warped mission to destroy Levi, but Blondie's misplaced belief that he were somehow trading higher in sexual currency than the spoilt rich kid annoyed Dwight for some reason.

*You need to be brought down a peg or two.*

"How badly do you want my cock?" Dwight said frankly.

"Really badly."

"Bad enough to let me own you?"

"Own me?"

"Yes. Own you."

Blondie coughed nervously. "What does that entail?"

Dwight lifted a wicked eyebrow, regarding himself in the rearview mirror. "If you're man enough to find out tell me where you are and I'll come get you."

# CHAPTER 2

*Tick. Tick. Tick.*

The imaginary sound of a ticking time bomb was all Levi could think of as he lay tied to the bed like a stick of dynamite, his fuse getting shorter and shorter, just waiting to explode. His heart pounded with a toxic blend of anger and extreme anxiety, his pulse thundering in his ears. He was a mess of hideous emotions. But he refused to cry. Fuck that. Nothing a lowlife like Dwight Stephenson did would ever make him shed a tear.

*Tick. Tick. Tick.*

"Just fucking get loose," he swore at the knots tying his wrists and feet to the corners of the bed. When they didn't obey his command he screamed in frustration. "FUUUCK!" This yelling out did him no favours because all it did was made him need to take deeper breaths, something he was trying not to do so he could avoid inhaling the musky ball sweat of his stepfather's underwear smothering his face.

*Tick. Tick. Tick.*

He didn't know how long he had until whoever Dwight had text would turn up and find him like this. It was imperative he break free; he couldn't let anyone find him in such a humiliating position. He had over a thousand contacts in his phone and didn't have the faintest clue who Dwight would have messaged. The only thing Levi could be sure of was that no matter who Dwight text none of them would expect to see this pathetic sight.

*Tick. Tick. Tick.*

As angry as he was with Dwight, Levi was more angry with himself for being stupid enough for trusting this man. Beneath the anger was colossal shame for calling Dwight his daddy. He still wasn't sure what it was that had triggered it but at some point in the middle of being pinned beneath Dwight's humping body Levi had found himself so turned on, so free, that he genuinely felt he'd found someone who could protect and love him in ways he'd never experienced before.

"Fucking get loose," Levi hissed at his hands, his wrists burning from the immense pulling he was doing. Dwight had only used shoe laces and t-shirts to tie him up with but the knots were so tight they refused to budge. Just as he thought he'd managed to loosen the knot around his right hand, he heard footsteps approaching his bedroom door. Levi was shaking, his heart trying to pound its way out of his chest. The door swung open and...

*BOOM!*

Levi's heart blew to smithereens and he knew it would never beat the same again. He broke out in a cold sweat all over his naked body, his stomach wobbling like toxic slime. Before the voice even spoke, Levi sensed who it was.

*No. No. No. No. No.*

"Oh my god," came the horrified whisper belonging to his best friend.

Levi bit his lip so hard it nearly drew blood. He should have fucking known Dwight would text Josh. They hadn't spoken since Josh's birthday weekend when Levi had sucked him off. It was always going to be awkward when they did finally talk again but this was taking that awkward to stratosphere levels of awkward.

The only thing he was grateful for was being tied face down so Josh couldn't see his deflated cock and shrivelled balls. He wasn't the biggest in the pants department at the best of times but he was even smaller now since his manhood had climbed inside itself after discovering he was being blindfolded with Mark's underwear. An irrational fear ran through his bones as he wondered if Josh would be able to tell that his arse had been fucked. He may have sucked Josh off but that had been under the pretence of bromance curiosity, if Josh knew a man had done this to him then Levi would have some explaining to do.

*Just tell him it was some crazy chick into kink.*

"Levi, are you okay?" Josh asked, his voice full of concern as he rushed over to the bed.

"I'm okay... just fucking untie me," Levi replied, sounding angrier than he meant to.

Josh immediately began working on the knots around Levi's right foot before moving to the left foot. When he finally untied one of Levi's hands Levi ripped his stepfather's underwear off his face and hurled them across the room like a grenade. He sucked in a deep breath of fresh air, desperate to cleanse himself of their putrid smell.

"I'm sorry I took so long to get here but I was at work when you text." Josh stared at him as he untied the last knot, his mind suddenly clicking that it can't have been Levi who sent the text. "Wait a minute. Who was it that text me?"

"Some idiot who thought it would be funny if you found me like this," Levi grumbled.

"Whoever they are needs a fucking punch. You don't tie someone up and leave them helpless."

Levi wondered if Josh would still be keen to punch who did this if he knew the person responsible was his father.

When Josh was finished with the last knot he took a step back and turned away to give Levi some privacy to get dressed. "Are you going to tell me what happened?" he asked as he stared out the window.

"Is it okay with you if I didn't?" Levi slipped on the first pair of briefs he could find. He stretched his arms out, flexing his wrists, grateful to be free. "You can turn around now."

Josh turned round slowly and faced him. His face still looked concerned but there was a hint of a smile there. "Whoever tied you up has definitely got some sharp fucking teeth judging by those hickeys."

"Fucking hell." Levi rubbed his neck marked with scandal. He didn't need a mirror to know how unsightly they must be.

Josh crinkled his nose. "Smells like a lot of sex went down here today." He inhaled loudly and chuckled. "Yep. Definitely a lot. I could almost get high off the fuck fumes."

Levi didn't say anything, avoiding making eye contact with his best mate. He was glad Josh was trying to make light of the situation but he was too embarrassed to join in with the joking just yet.

Josh flicked his gaze around the room. "So who was *he*?"

"It wasn't a he," Levi hissed.

"Come on, man. You can tell me. You know I don't care about that sort of thing."

"What makes you think it was a guy?" Levi rubbed his heels together nervously.

Josh pointed at Levi's back. "Because I don't think a girl would write something like that."

Levi's stomach dropped to his toes. He'd forgotten about Dwight writing on him. He shuffled over to the mirror by his wardrobe and glanced over his shoulder to see what Dwight had marked him with.

*You fucking prick!*

In huge black letters across his lower back were the words **CUM BUCKET.** Levi fired a glob of spit into his palm and used his saliva to try and rub it off but it barely smudged the letters. "For fucks sake."

Josh picked up a t-shirt off the floor and went and stood behind him. "Let me help." He pressed the shirt to Levi's back and rubbed firmly, trying to work Levi's saliva into the skin and help erase the derogatory message. His free hand held Levi's shoulder as he applied more pressure to the bold letters, scrubbing roughly. The touch of Josh's hand made Levi's skin crawl. Not that Josh was disgusting—he was fucking perfect—but because Levi himself felt disgusting.

"It's not coming off sorry, buddy. I think you'll find this is a hot shower and soap job."

"I think you could be right," Levi mumbled. He could feel Josh's breath warm upon his neck and it should have felt great but it just didn't. Dwight had killed off any sexual urges Levi had left.

Levi now realised why Dwight had text his own son to be the one to come release him. There was no unseeing the corrupted sight of Levi tied to the bed and for the rest of their friendship Josh would always know about today. The younger Stephenson would also be on high alert around Levi from now on, no more being susceptible to innocent sexual exploring. If Levi were to ever make a subtle move then Josh would know Levi was anything but innocent when it came to gay stuff. Dwight was making sure his son was safe from ever being a Candy Boy story.

Josh dropped the shirt and stepped away. "So who was it?" he asked again.

Levi sighed. He wanted to tell Josh but he knew he couldn't. Dwight had that hidden camera with the footage. He couldn't risk irking Dwight's wraith and have him doing something stupid like showing people what was on that video—which he very well might do if he found out Levi had ratted on him to his own son.

"Are you at least going to confirm it was a guy who did this?" Josh began to look surly.

"What's the big deal if it's a guy or a girl. You said yourself you don't care."

"And I don't care… but I do care if you don't trust me enough to be honest with me." Josh's sweet brown eyes glimmered with hurt. "You're my best mate. We're not supposed to have secrets. I tell you everything."

That was true. Levi knew Josh's deepest and darkest secrets, which weren't all that deep or dark. And that is exactly why he was so careful with what he shared with Josh. The dark-blond stud was a genuinely nice guy and it didn't feel right to corrupt someone so good with such ugly truths.

"Fine. If you don't trust me then forget about it," Josh said snottily, making his way towards the door.

Levi panicked seeing his best mate leaving, abandoning him. "It-it was a guy," he spluttered. "I got tied up, blindfolded with dirty underwear, and fucked by a guy. Two guys actually. One of them didn't use a condom which is why I have cum bucket written on my back."

Josh spun around, his eyes bugging. "You have cum in you right now?"

"That's all you have to say?"

Josh laughed. "Sorry. I'm just… just a bit shocked. Not in a bad way, just… shocked." He smiled. "But do you?"

Levi rolled his eyes. "Yes, Josh. I have cum inside me."

"Whoa, that's pretty intense."

"You're telling me."

"And two guys?"

"Yep. Two guys," Levi said through gritted teeth, wishing he knew the identity of the mystery man whose cum was deep inside him.

Josh schooled his expression to serious and pinned Levi with cool dark eyes. "You should know better than to do unsafe stuff like that."

"Thank you, Doctor Stephenson, I do know that."

"Then why did you do it?" Josh demanded, glaring icily. "You don't let just anybody do that sort of thing."

The unblinking scrutiny made Levi squirm. "I know, I know. I'm sorry. It was just one of those moments, you know." He smiled, masking his true anger at being fucked raw by a total stranger. "Too damn horny for my own good."

Josh sighed, dropping his parental scorn. "Yeah, man. I know exactly what you mean. I can be the same sometimes." He chuckled before quickly adding, "But with girls."

Josh might have been understanding but even he didn't want any confusion about his sexual preferences.

Levi nodded. "So are we all good?"

"Yeah, man. We're fine. I don't care who you sleep with."

Levi knew the answer to his next question but he wanted to ask it anyway. "You won't tell anyone about today, will you?"

"I won't say a word. I promise." The look of sincerity on Josh's face filled Levi with warmth. His best mate would keep his secret.

"Thanks, man."

"No worries," Josh said.

Levi wondered if now would be a good time to address the awkwardness of the birthday blowjob but he decided against it. He'd been through enough uncomfortable moments for one day.

"Sorry that you had to be dragged from work to come untie me," Levi said.

"What are best mates for?" Josh tilted his head thoughtfully. "So who are these two arseholes that left you tied up?"

"You won't know them."

"Are you sure? Fitzroy is only so big."

"I'm sure."

Josh wouldn't let up. "You never know, I might know them. Just tell me their names." His brown eyes turned disproving. "Unless of course you don't know their names."

"Of course I know their bloody names." *Well, one of them.* "I just don't want to get into it with you... I'm embarrassed enough if you couldn't tell."

"Sorry, bro," Josh said softly, backing off. "But that is scummy to leave someone tied up like that. If I ever saw them I'd knock them both out for you."

Levi's heart skipped a beat. Hearing the usually level-headed Josh sound so protective of him was wonderful. "Thanks, man." A brief pause settled over the room before Levi added, "Well, um, I won't hold you up. I'm fine now so you can head back to work."

"Not so fast. There's something I gotta do before I go."

"What's that?"

A smile bloomed on Josh's lips. "Come here." He stepped towards Levi with his arms open wide.

"Shit, do we really need to hug this one out?" Levi said, cringing. "You're wearing your deli uniform and probably smell of ham."

"Yeah, and you stink of sex so who cares."

Levi laughed. "Touché."

"Now give me my bloody hug," Josh demanded.

"Why the fuck do you need a hug?"

"Because I want you to know I have no problem with you being who you are." He wrapped his strong arms around Levi, squeezing a little too tight. "I love you, man."

"Ditto." The word escaped Levi in a whisper. He half-shivered, conscious of his bare chest pressing against Josh's strong torso, their crotches almost touching while Josh's stubble scratched Levi's neck.

"Call me later tonight, okay?"

"Will do." Levi let go of Josh before he started crying. He may not have been prepared to shed a tear for Dwight's darkness but Josh's light risked ripping the lid off Levi's emotions.

As soon as he was alone, Levi wandered over to his closet and stood and stared at the white shirt hanging in his closet. The smears of dried blood down the front gave away its sinister past. It was the one thing in the world that was proof it wasn't wise to mess with Levi Candy.

His need for revenge burned like hot embers in his throat. He didn't know what it was he would do to Dwight Stephenson just yet, but tonight the pair would be coming face to face to settle the score once and for all. The only thing Levi did know was that he would be coming home with a victory.

# CHAPTER 3

*Eight hours later*

"Enjoying yourself?" Dwight grunted, spanking Blondie's smooth arse. He liked how boyish the brat's body was and how his sporty physique radiated youth from head to toe. Despite the boy's deep voice, hairy muscled legs, and springy brown pubes growing above a slightly-curved six-inch cock, Dwight knew Blondie had not owned masculine traits for long. If he had a time machine and went back just three or four years Dwight knew he would find a scrawny teen a few inches shorter most likely suffering from acne.

"Yes, Daddy," Blondie panted.

Dwight snorted derisively, giving another slap. "Listen to you, calling me daddy after making fun of Soggy for doing the same thing." He bit the boy's earlobe. "You're such a pathetic little slut. Isn't that right, bitch?" He dragged his cock out and slammed back in.

Blondie whimpered, burying his face into the seat of the couch and lifted his arse higher. "Yeah," he mumbled.

"Yeah, what?"

"Yes, Daddy. I'm pathetic."

The tone of the boy's voice gave away his annoyance at being called out for the pathetic slut he was being turned into but Dwight didn't care; he just kept spanking, grunting, and fucking.

He didn't know why he'd demanded Blondie call him Daddy. Maybe he hoped it would replicate the intensity of the sex he'd shared with Levi earlier. It wasn't working though. Blondie was nothing but a cheap substitute.

He'd been fucking the boy's arse on and off all evening under the guise of teaching him how to be a better bottom but all Dwight had really done was obliterate the boy's sphincter with selfish fuck-punches. The kid wasn't doing too badly considering being bottom wasn't his preferred role but he was so damn cock-struck he embraced whatever Dwight dished out.

Being cock-struck was a dangerous thing, Dwight thought. It made you do things you normally wouldn't do, things you knew you shouldn't do. All men were guilty of thinking with their cock on occasion but when you were cock-struck then that was a case of your brain taking up fulltime residence in your pants. Had Dwight not done what he'd done to Levi then there was every chance he would have been in the same boat Blondie was right now, following his cock's wishes and stupidly thinking it had something to do with his heart. Fuck that for a joke. There was no way Dwight was ever going to let a stuck up prick like Levi Candy rule his heart.

"Ohhh, Daddy," Blondie cried out. "You're so fucking big!"

"Yeah, that's it, slut. You take this big dick." Dwight cast his eyes down, watching his shaft glide in and out Blondie's overstretched rectum. "You hungry-holed bitch."

Blondie gasped, slipping a hand between his legs to play with himself.

"No you don't," Dwight growled, yanking Blondie's hand away. "Your little cock belongs to me now. I decide when you can play with it."

"Sorry, Daddy."

Dwight shoved the boy's face into the seat of the couch while burying his own face in Blondie's golden locks. He bit at his nape and thrust a few more times, whispering dirty and degrading words in his ear. He was at the point where he could shoot his load if he wanted but he held back his orgasm, preferring to drag Blondie's ordeal out a bit longer.

"My arse needs a break, Daddy," Blondie said shakily, his voice cracking as Dwight jabbed his cock deep. "Please?"

Dwight sighed like the kid was asking for the world. "Alright, but just a quick one." Pulling his bare cock slowly out of Blondie's body, he savoured the way the boy's stretched, wet hole gaped at first before slowly contracting.

"You definitely know how to fuck," Blondie panted.

"And you definitely know how to take a cock."

Blondie's cheeks pinked. "Apparently so," he whispered.

Dwight sat up on the couch, reached for his packet of Marlboro lights and lit himself a smoke.

Blondie uncurled his body and sat on the floor beside Dwight's feet. "I can't believe you own me now, Daddy," he said, his voice laced with awe.

Dwight nodded, exhaling a cloud of smoke. "I sure do. You have the tattoo to prove it."

Blondie reached behind his back, gently dabbing his fingers over his new tattoo painted just above his arse crack. It was a small and simple but effective design; Dwight's initials *DS* in red and yellow ink. It wasn't exactly a pretty design but that hadn't been the point, Dwight had just wanted something that signified Blondie was now his property.

The kid had been reluctant at first, shaking his head and saying "No fucking way" when Dwight first suggested it. But when Dwight threatened to drive off and never see him again the kid cracked, agreeing to being marked for life. Since leaving the tattoo parlour though, Blondie had been surprisingly upbeat about the ugly tattoo, saying again and again how much he liked it. Dwight suspected the kid would like it a lot less in a few days when he realised it wasn't something he could just wash off.

"Regretting it?" Dwight asked.

"No. I really like it," Blondie scrambled to say. "But what do I tell people when they see it?"

"DS can stand for many things. Dumb Slut, Dwight's slut, dick sucker."

Blondie laughed but edgily.

"Tell them it's a personal thing," Dwight suggested. "It's nobody's business but yours what you do with your body."

"Yeah… that's true." The kid didn't sound convinced. "Am I the first person who's ever gotten a tattoo for you?"

"Yep," Dwight grunted.

Blondie's face glowed with pride, probably thinking he was special. Too bad for him that he wasn't. Dwight had lied. There were several faggots up in Auckland wandering about with tattoos paying homage to Dwight Stephenson, each design a little different but each one containing his initials in some form or another. They had been hardcore submissives he'd met through seedy sex clubs, usually off their face on meth at the time and more than willing to offer up their flesh. One guy had been covered with names, barcodes and phrases already, his body a canvas for the scribblings of sadistic men who liked to leave their mark.

Blondie began to stroke the hairs above Dwight's ankle, his gaze pointed at Dwight with pure adulation.

21

Dwight kicked the boy's hand away. "Stop being such a girl. If you wanna do something nice for me then you can tongue my balls while I finish my smoke."

"Yes, Daddy." Blondie scooted over to sit between Dwight's spread legs, craned his neck low, and proceeded to lick Dwight's hairy sac. Dwight shuddered when the boy slurped one whole ball in his mouth, sucking wildly.

"Thatta boy. Suck those big balls for me."

Blondie hummed affirmatively, slurping across to Dwight's other ball.

Dwight looked down at his deflating dick resting over Blondie's face. The boy was gazing up at him from his mouthful of nutsack. Dwight smiled back then carelessly flicked the ash of his cigarette onto Blondie's back, chuckling. "Isn't it funny to think you told me you were a top when we first met. Yet here you are being my bitch."

Blondie pulled off and rocked back on his heels, drooling and smiling. "I'm proud to be your bitch."

"I'm talking about you, not to you." Dwight shoved the boy's face back between his legs. "Keep sucking."

Blondie scowled but he did what he was told, sucking Dwight's balls like he was putting out a fire. When Dwight had smoked his cigarette down to the filter, he leaned over Blondie and stubbed it out in the ashtray then sat back and lifted his legs and rested them over Blondie's shoulders. "Now my arsehole."

Blondie spat Dwight's nuts out. "What?"

"Lick my arse out."

"But…"

"Is there a problem?" A disgruntled scowl thinned Dwight's lips.

"I've never rimmed anyone before." Blondie's panicky breath blew heated over Dwight's dick.

"I would say now's a good time to start."

It was obvious Blondie wanted to argue, but Dwight's hard, domineering glare silenced any protest about to be made. The boy grimaced, eyeing the dark crevice of Dwight's hairy crack. He slowly lifted his hands, parting the flesh of Dwight's buttocks to expose his anus.

"So… I just lick it, right?" Blondie kept staring at Dwight's hole.

"That's right."

Dwight's arsehole was a no-go zone when it came to fingers and dicks but it was very welcoming of wet tongues. One of his favourite things to do was to tie his lovers up and sit on their face and force them to tongue his steamy crack, and if Blondie didn't start licking then that is exactly what Dwight would be doing to him.

"Fucking lick it already, bitch," Dwight barked angrily.

Blondie closed his eyes and lowered his mouth, his tongue gently petting around Dwight's hole in pitiful dabs. Dwight dug his heels into Blondie's back and grabbed the back of his head, demanding the boy lick harder. "Lick it like a man. I want my hole dripping with spit."

Blondie pressed his tongue deeper, digging into Dwight's anal trench. He mumbled an unpleasant sound, probably in response to the unpleasant taste.

"That's it," Dwight moaned as he watched the blond head between his legs. "Now start licking up and down."

Blondie licked up and down the length of Dwight's hairy crack, each pass over his hole getting a little more forceful and jabby.

Dwight shivered and chuckled. "Ye-Yeah, that's it, Blondie. You know it. The more you clean it the better it will taste."

Blondie took his advice, wildly slobbering over Dwight's hole, corkscrewing his tongue right over Dwight's

23

shitter, desperately trying to fuck him with his tongue—which was never gonna happen, Dwight was far too tight. Still, Blondie kept trying, swirling and jabbing and gnawing at Dwight's rim like it was a hot meal. It wasn't a great rimjob, it was actually quite crap, but it was still a rimjob, one of the few sex acts a person didn't need to be good at it to still be able to gift immense pleasure.

Dwight's toes curled and his eyes began to shudder, shivers of bliss shooting up and down his spine. *Fuck this feels good.* He was quite happy to just lay back and enjoy this arse-licking treatment for the rest of the night if he could but he knew he'd have to get back to fucking the boy at some point.

When Dwight was satisfied Blondie had given his hole a thorough tongue bath, he pushed him away with his feet. "Right, let's take you to the bedroom and finish fucking that hole of yours."

Blondie wiped his mouth clean and got to his feet, following Dwight to his bedroom like an obedient puppy.

"Bend over the end of the bed," Dwight ordered as he walked to the wardrobe.

Blondie dropped to his knees and draped his chest over the mattress.

Dwight eyed his many toys, inspecting the various sized dildos available to him. He loved using his cock as the main weapon to stretch an arsehole open but he wasn't deluded when it came to the size of his cock. He would tell people online his dick was 7.5 to 8 inches but in reality he was only a whisker over 7. His meat was long and thick enough to stretch a body good but it wasn't exactly arse-breaking material. If Blondie was going to become a regular then that meant he had to be loosened up much more. Dwight didn't like to just fuck his sluts, he liked to wreck their arses. It wasn't going to happen overnight but Dwight fully expected to have Blondie taking his fist before too long.

"What's in there?" Blondie asked.

"Just a few toys to help make the evening more fun."

"What sort of toys?"

"Never you mind. Just stay bent over the bed."

"Yes, Daddy."

Dwight grabbed some rope and a ball gag from the top shelf then walked over and casually went about tying Blondie's wrists to the bottom bedposts.

"Kinky," Blondie said, wriggling his restrained wrists. "I've never been tied up before."

"Stick with me and you will end up doing lots of things you've never done before."

"Fuck yeah. I can't wait." The youthful enthusiasm of Blondie's voice was sweet, albeit misguided.

Dwight wondered sometimes what was wrong with people who so willingly allowed themselves to be tied up and put themselves at the mercy of a total stranger. Blondie might have had Dwight's name tattooed on him but the kid barely knew Dwight. All they had shared was a ballsy fuck in a tavern's toilets and then the dubious scenario of raping Levi together.

*It wasn't rape!* Dwight's mind shouted. *It was a lesson that needed to be taught.*

"Open up," Dwight said, jamming the ball gag in Blondie's mouth and strapping it in place. He patted the back of the boy's head and said, "How's that feel?"

Blondie mumbled back; his words indecipherable as he drooled down his chin.

"Perfect." Dwight grinned. "Now let's see what I can use to fuck your arse with."

Blondie moaned loudly, shaking the bedposts.

"Settle down, bitch. I ain't gonna shove anything too extreme up there. Just something a little bigger than my dick."

Blondie mumbled again, something that sounded a bit like, "Okay, Daddy."

Dwight walked back to the wardrobe, perusing his options. In the end he settled on a lifelike veined dildo about the same length as his own cock but about an inch thicker. "This should do the trick." He knelt down behind Blondie's imprisoned body, spat on his fingers and rubbed two of them over the boy's hole. Blondie's eager hole winked open from the touch of his fingers, swallowing them to the knuckle.

Blondie groaned pleasurably as Dwight gently finger-fucked him, his feet widening apart as if he were inviting Dwight deeper into his private places. Dwight continued the soft fingering, kissing the tattoo on Blondie's back as he gifted the boy a rare touch of affection.

Placing the dildo to Blondie's entrance, Dwight said, "Here it comes." He pressed the tip of the dildo inside the boy's slick anal lips, the device sliding in with ease until it got halfway—the thickest section of the life-like cock. Blondie whimpered and gripped the bedposts in white knuckled fists, mumbling loudly as his arsehole did all it could to push back against the silicone intrusion. Dwight chuckled. "Stop resisting, slut. It's going in if you like it or not."

Blondie didn't listen, his wriggling backside trying to break free but it was a losing battle, Dwight just pushed harder, forcing the dildo deeper inside and expanding the limits of the boy's arsehole.

He stroked the nape of the boy's neck. "Just relax, Blondie." His tone was sensual and caring, a complete polar opposite of what was happening to the boy's arse. "You just relax and take it. Daddy's got to get this all in."

He cringed when he realised he'd referred to himself as daddy. It didn't feel right. Not the way it had with Levi. *Just another reason why you needed to cut ties with the sneaky fucker.*

Blondie let out one helluva loud growl, his hands violently pulling at the bedposts as Dwight forced the last two inches inside him.

"Chill out, Blondie. It's all in now. Just relax and let your arsehole adjust to it."

Blondie whimpered, his back heaving up and down like rolling waves.

Dwight shuffled backwards to admire his handywork. The boy's arse was jampacked with fake dick, stretched to full capacity. He decided he'd chosen the perfect size. Any smaller and it wouldn't have expanded the kid enough, any more and it would have caused bleeding. Dwight just sat and stared for a few minutes, waiting for Blondie's breathing to return to normal.

He'd had regular male fucks in the past but they had all been Auckland based, Blondie would be his first on-call faggot who lived in the same region. That would have its benefits but it also had its risks. As long as Blondie knew how to keep his mouth shut then they would be fine, and if the kid was as in the closet as he claimed to be then it shouldn't be a problem.

Dwight tickled the sole of one of Blondie's feet, making the boy flinch and jerk his foot about. Dwight chuckled, gripping Blondie by the ankle and dishing out a torturous long series of tickles. "This is fun," he teased. "I love seeing you squirm."

Blondie mumbled out a giggle.

When Dwight was done playing nice, he gripped the base of the dildo and went about reshaping Blondie's fuck-hole to the loose orifice he craved. Immediately, Blondie regripped the bedposts, moaning and spluttering spitty hisses over the gag each time the dildo pulled at his clasping anal lips. Just as Dwight was onto his fifth full-length plunge, a series of pulsating knocks erupted from the front door.

"Whoever the fuck that is has terrible timing," he muttered, carelessly ramming the dildo back in. He seriously contemplated not answering the door but considering the lights were all on and his Ute was out front it would be a little too obvious he was home. Rather than risk whoever it was just walking inside and finding him fucking another dude, Dwight decided it was best to go see who it was.

He got to his feet and walked over to a pile of dirty laundry in the corner of his room, he pulled on a pair of jeans and picked up a pair of briefs that he went and slid over Blondie's head. "You can sniff on these while I'm gone. And no making any noise." He gave Blondie a slap on the arse and went to go answer the door.

# CHAPTER 4

Levi was trembling so much he could barely lift his hand to knock on the door and when he did, his fist pounded the door much harder than he'd intended. *What am I doing here?* He kept asking himself. *You are here to deal to the prick.* That was it. He was here to demand an apology and the name of the mystery man who seeded him.

It had been over eight hours since Josh had untied him and Levi was still in shock from what had happened. He felt like he'd just walked away from a high-speed car crash, his body aching and his mind fuzzy. He knew he probably should have stayed at home and waited to clear his head before doing anything rash, like driving forty minutes to Rapanui Beach to accost his best friend's father, but he had an urge to get even.

*Just be cool. Just be cool. You're always cool*, Levi told himself.

He usually was cool and calm but what had happened was not something he could easily put to the back of his mind. It wasn't just the degrading humiliation of being entered by a man he didn't know that upset him, he was also upset about how he'd allowed Dwight to witness his most private and dark desires. Desires Levi didn't even know he had in his heart until the older man had unlocked them.

*That is so fucking embarrassing. I can't believe I called him Daddy.* Not only had he called Dwight daddy but he had fucking loved doing it, loved it so much that each time he'd said the term of endearment his cock had twitched and leaked tears of precum joy.

*And now he fucking pays.* How exactly he was going to make Dwight pay was not something Levi had quite figured out yet but standing and screaming at him, maybe even kicking the fucker in the nuts, would be a good start. He wasn't leaving here until Dwight Stephenson had apologised and accepted responsibility for the evil act he had done.

"I'm coming," Dwight called out, his thumping footsteps getting closer until the outside light switched on. The door swung open and Dwight appeared in just a pair of jeans, his hairy chest glistening with a light sheen of sweat. A hank of hair hung over one of his eyes, his expression unreadable. "What are you doing here, Soggy?"

Levi suppressed the voice in his head demanding he punch the bastard in his handsome face. "You…" his loud voice trailed off. "You…" he repeated, but again his voice drowned out like it had stage fright. He dropped his gaze to Dwight's bare feet.

Dwight huffed out a quick breath, blowing his messy fringe out of his eyes. "Spit it out, Soggy. I haven't got all fucking night."

Levi drew his eyes from Dwight's toes to his soulful eyes, pausing for an extra beat on the crotch of his jeans, the virile terrain of his muscular chest. He wasn't just sexy, he was beautiful, too. It suddenly dawned on Levi: he wasn't here for revenge, he was here for forgiveness.

"I'm sorry," Levi said.

Dwight stared back, incredulous. "What did you say?"

"I'm sorry." Levi tried smiling. "I want to apologise for the hidden camera. I shouldn't have done that."

Dwight chewed his lip in concentration. "No, you shouldn't have."

"I deserved—" Levi's voice broke, and he tried again. "I deserved the punishment."

Dwight yawned, stretching his arms. "Well, Soggy, cheers for apologising. That's big of you. Now if you don't mind, I'm going back to bed."

"That's it?"

"Yep. That's it."

"But I just said sorry."

"Were you after a medal or something?"

"Not a medal but maybe an invite inside."

"And why would you want to come inside?" Dwight stared back, and one of his brows ticked up.

"I don't know… to have a chat?"

Dwight narrowed his eyes, suspicion brewing in his pupils. "So you can then knife me in the back more like it."

"What? Why would I do that?"

"Despite the fact I was well within my rights to do what I did to you today, I know that there is no way in hell that you—Mr up-his-own-arse—would actually come here to apologise. You're here to try and pull a swifty on me and quite frankly, Soggy, I'm not in the fucking mood. Just go grab a rock and throw it through one of my windows if you think it will make you feel better, but once you've done that I suggest you turn around, get in your car, and go home and just stay away from me."

"You're right, I did come here to have you up about what you did but now I…" Levi paused, struggling to decide between obeying his pride or his cock. His pride should have taken priority but Dwight's body was speaking to him in ways he couldn't ignore.

"Spit it out, Soggy, I haven't got all fucking night."

"I want you to fuck me again." Even though it was exactly what he wanted to say, Levi couldn't quite believe he'd said it. "I am willing to forget all about today if you are. Just let me feel you inside me again."

Dwight glanced down the hallway then turned back to meet Levi's gaze. "You mean that?"

"Yes, daddy." *Fuck that feels good to say again.*

"You're really into this daddy shit, aren't you?"

"That's because I'm into you."

Dwight stared back with a cocky and somewhat contemptuous smile. "Have you still got Blondie's cum inside you?"

"Who is Blondie?"

"The guy who fucked you."

"I know that but what's his name?"

"His name is Blondie," Dwight said sternly. "Now answer my question. Do you still have his cum inside you?"

Levi wasn't sure if there was a right or wrong answer so he just told the truth. "I got rid of most of it but I can still feel some of him inside me."

That brought a smile to Dwight's lips.

"Are you keen?" Levi asked. "To fuck me?"

Dwight scratched his stomach, taking his time to reply. "I will fuck you but it has to be quick. I wanna go to bed soon."

Levi stepped inside, about to head to the lounge, but Dwight put an arm across the door, blocking the way.

"Not so fast. We fuck here."

"Here?" Levi frowned. "Right at the front door?"

"We fuck here, or not at all." Dwight's dark eyes sizzled with authority.

"Okay, Daddy. You're the boss."

"That's right," Dwight said. "Now take off your clothes."

Levi scuffed off his shoes and quickly removed his clothes. He gripped his dick, squeezing his manhood that was swelling fast.

"And your socks," Dwight said. "I like my boys fully naked."

Levi peeled his socks off, giving himself to Dwight the way the older man wanted.

"You weren't lying about wanting me to fuck you." Dwight's gaze pointed at Levi's growing erection. "You must really have it bad for me."

"Like you wouldn't believe."

Dwight reached out and gripped Levi's cock, squeezing hard. "This little pecker still hasn't fucked an arse yet, has it?"

"Not a guy's arse."

Dwight gave Levi's cock a firm tug. "That's probably just as well. You're too small to waste your time being a top."

Levi knew Dwight's statement was untrue but he didn't argue. If Dwight enjoyed mocking his perfectly adequate six inches then so be it. "I'm happy to be whatever you want me to be, daddy."

"I wrote on your body what I want you to be."

Levi shivered, partly from fear, partly from anticipation. "Do you want to cum inside me?"

"Yup." Dwight released his grip on Levi's dick. "But you can suck my cock a bit first."

Levi sank to the floor and without being asked, he planted a servile kiss on each of Dwight's size 11 feet, making sure the man knew just how much Levi respected him.

Dwight snickered and said, "Who's your daddy, Soggy?"

"You're my daddy, Sir! Dwight Stephenson is my daddy!"

"What is it you like about me so much?"

"Everything, Daddy. Everything."

Dwight's amused smile turned into a superior smirk. "Fuck yeah. Now get to work." He hauled his semi-erect dick out of his jeans and rammed it in Levi's mouth, causing Levi to gag.

Dwight's dick tasted funky, a mix of sweat, sex, and arse. *He mustn't have showered since he fucked me,* Levi thought but that didn't stop him from servicing his daddy's dick with the respect it deserved. He sucked hard and firm, plunging up and down Dwight's thick shaft in hungry, sloppy slurps. He slipped a hand inside the gap of Dwight's fly and began to fondle the older man's meaty balls, making sure he gifted Dwight as much pleasure as possible. He tried tugging Dwight's jeans down with his other hand, hungry to stroke his bare legs but Dwight swatted his hand away, only allowing Levi access through his open zipper.

Dwight was grunting softly and looking down at Levi as he sucked him. He held Levi's head tightly in place and started face-fucking him. With a firm grip on Levi's head, Dwight moved him around as he pleased while bucking his hips. Dwight steadily fucked his throat, pulling Levi's face all the way to his sweaty crotch, leaving his dick to soak for a few seconds, and then forcefully angling his head back for better access to his willing throat.

"Look at you, bitch." Dwight laughed. "You just love sucking a real man's cock, don't you?"

Levi tried replying but his response came out as a dick-sucking garble.

"Fucking faggot," Dwight sniggered.

Each nasty word and each thrust of Dwight's dick in his mouth was a punch to Levi's pride. He didn't care though. He was getting high on being treated so low. There was something comforting about the ridicule and being reminded of his place—beneath that of a *real* man—and while it wasn't the kindest place to be it was at least a safe one. But there was more to this. Much more. Levi sensed that beneath Dwight's cocky, cutting bravado lie a wealth of affection. It was buried deep inside Dwight's heart but if Levi could dig it out then it would be worth more than all the treasure in the world.

Dwight suddenly pulled Levi's mouth off his cock. "It's time to fuck," he grunted. He grabbed Levi by his hair and dragged him to his feet before turning him around and pressing his face against the wall.

Levi raised his hands, resting them either side of his head, and spread his legs wide like he was about to be strip-searched. He wasn't sure what to expect but it wasn't the rushed entrance Dwight made after a pitiful amount of spit was rubbed on Levi's still-tender anus.

"Easy, Daddy, easy," Levi pleaded.

Dwight didn't listen, sinking in to the hilt.

Levi's pained yelp was silenced by Dwight's right hand pinning his lips shut. "Keep ya voice down, Soggy," he muttered. "I want a quick fuck. Not a noisy one." He pulled his cock back to the tip and sank all the way back in, ripping Levi's sphincter to shreds. He kept doing it, pulling nearly all the way out before slamming right back in, not giving Levi any say in the raunchy rhythm their bodies began to dance to.

In. Out. In. Out.

Shallow. Deep. Shallow. Deep.

Rough. Rough. Rough. Rough.

Levi refused to let the pain invading his body push away his pleasure. He wanted both to live within him in equal measure. Dwight supplied the hurt but he also supplied the remedy, his unfiltered moans of passion acted like a pacifier, encouraging Levi to hang in there and accept the pain. The hurt was worth it if it meant he could hear his daddy gain pleasure from his body and fill him with a liquid reward.

Dwight's ragged breaths soaked his ear while desire burned between them in a brazen heat, untamed and ravenous. Levi thought they were at the start of a marathon but Dwight was true to his word and only after a sprint. Within two minutes, Dwight's body went rigid and he bit down on Levi's neck as his dick spasmed inside Levi's arsehole. The older man's dick kept shooting, shooting, shooting until his balls had emptied completely, turning Levi's arse into a lake of sperm for the second time that day.

Levi embraced the warmth of Dwight's seed inside him, grateful to be receiving.

Dwight yanked his dick out, tapping Levi on the shoulder. "Clean me," he whispered hoarsely.

Levi turned around and sank to his knees, plopping Dwight's dick in his mouth and sucking it clean. He couldn't believe what he was doing but he treated it like an honour, eager to respect the dick that had just claimed him so fully. When he was done, Levi got to his feet and tried to give Dwight a kiss.

Dwight grimaced, stepping back.

"What's wrong, daddy?"

"I can't kiss you."

"Why?"

"Aside from the fact I don't want to kiss a bloke whose just cleaned his own arse off my cock, I don't kiss used goods."

"Used goods?"

"You're used goods, Soggy. I told you that earlier today after Blondie spunked inside you. And now you've let me as well. No offense, but I don't kiss cum buckets."

Levi blinked, more confused than angry by what Dwight was saying. "I didn't exactly have a say in what Blondie did to me though, did I?"

Dwight shrugged. "I don't make the rules, Soggy."

"Yes you do. You just made up that one."

"Look, I'm happy to fuck you now and then. No issues with that. I'm just saying I won't be kissing you anymore." He coughed up a smile and patted Levi on the rump. "I'm gonna go to bed now so how about you put your clothes back on and trot off."

"Trot off? You fuck me raw and then expect me to just 'trot off?'"

"What if the next time you come visiting with Joshy I'll let you sneak into my room when he's gone to bed. How's that sound?" Dwight shot him a condescending smile like he was doing Levi the biggest favour in the world.

Levi gave being nice one more shot. "Can I please have a kiss, Daddy? Just a quick one?" He knew how desperate he sounded but he needed the kiss. Without the kiss then what just happened felt dirty, made him feel like he was worthless.

Dwight raked a hand through his mussed hair. "Look, son. Quit with the daddy shit. I've dropped my load. I suggest you go home and have a wank. I find that helps us guys come to our senses."

"But Daddy…"

"Come on, Soggy. Pull yourself together. This isn't the Levi I know. You're beginning to freak me out."

"You made me a new Levi, that's why."

"Soggy just go home." Dwight's gaze pointed at the floor. "I don't want your arse leaking cum on my carpet."

Levi gaped, totally shocked at being spoken to like an un-toilet-trained cat. Just as he was about to scold Dwight for being so dismissive, a spluttering cough came from somewhere down the hall.

"Do you have somebody else here?" Levi asked suspiciously.

"I think you're imagining things, Soggy." Dwight gently pushed him in the direction of his clothes on the floor.

Another spluttering cough sounded, this time louder, followed by the unmistakable *thump* of something falling on the floor.

"I definitely just heard someone," Levi said.

"Soggy. Be a good boy for Daddy and go home."

Levi walked past Dwight and headed towards his bedroom.

"Oi, no you don't." Dwight grabbed his arm, trying to pull him back but Levi slipped free, accidentally whacking him in the guts.

Dwight keeled over, gasping for breath.

Levi stumbled towards Dwight's bedroom and opened the door. "What the fuck?"

He couldn't believe what he was seeing. Hunched over and tied to the end of Dwight's bed was a naked man with a flesh-coloured dildo on the floor between his legs. The man's arsehole was puffy and red and gaping wide, leaving Levi under no illusion as to where the dildo had just been. His lower back was marked by a bright red and yellow tattoo that spelt out the letters **DS**. Levi lifted his gaze and saw that the young man's head was covered with underwear, scraggly bits of blond hair poked out the side. *Blondie!* Levi went to step inside the room and pull the underwear off his face but just as he stepped forward he was tackled to the floor by a grunting Dwight.

"I fucking told you to get out of my house," Dwight growled, wrestling Levi away from Blondie.

Levi tried desperately to shove Dwight away but it was no use, Dwight had sprung to his feet and grabbed Levi by both his hands and dragged him violently up the hallway kicking and screaming.

"Let me go!" Levi yelled. "Let me go you arsehole."

Dwight dragged him over the threshold of the front door, dumping him on the front porch before stepping back inside and guarding the entrance.

Levi scrambled to his feet, scowling. "You fucking prick! You just fucked me when you have someone else here."

"We aren't dating, Soggy, so don't go acting like a bitch about it."

Levi glowered, heated breaths hissing out of his mouth. "You were fucking him before I got here, weren't you?"

"Yeah, and?"

"You made me suck you off." Levi grimaced. "Sucked you off after your dick's been inside him"

Dwight chuckled. "I know. Pretty gross, aye?"

Levi lost it and threw a punch. His fist grazed Dwight's cheek, connecting just enough to make Dwight grunt. He went to storm back inside but Dwight shoved him back outside.

"You get one hit with me, Soggy. Just one. If you touch me again, I will fucking deck you."

"Just give me my fucking clothes, cunt."

Dwight slowly and carefully knelt down to pick up Levi's pants while keeping an eye on Levi the whole time, not giving him any chance to step a foot inside. He rose to his full height and pulled Levi's car keys out of the pants pocket and threw them down in front of Levi's feet. "Now fuck off."

"I asked for my clothes, not just my keys."

"Maybe you should have thought about that before punching me."

"GIVE ME MY FUCKING CLOTHES YOU RAPING CUNT!"

Dwight laughed. "Scream all you like, Soggy, but I have no neighbours anywhere near me who can hear your little bitch cries of the night."

Levi made a stance like he was about to charge inside but Dwight stomped his foot and raised his fist. "I'm warning you, faggot. One foot over this line and you'll be leaving here in an ambulance if I don't decide to bury you in the garden."

Despite being gripped with fury, Levi's inner survival instinct was stronger. He knew he was no match for Dwight physically, that would be a losing battle if ever there was one. He took a shaky breath and heaved out, "Just give me back my clothes."

"You had a chance to leave with them but you lost it. A bit like how you lost your dignity."

"Give me my fucking clothes."

Dwight ignored the demand. "I want you to take your leaky arse and that pathetic excuse for a cock of yours off my property."

"At least give me my fucking pants, Dwight."

Dwight shook his head. "If you don't leave here right now then I will make sure everyone you know sees that sexy video I have of you begging for my daddy dick."

Dread curled in Levi's stomach. "You wouldn't dare!"

Dwight smiled. "Good night, Soggy. I hope you have fun shitting me out." He slammed the door in Levi's face and switched off the outside light.

Levi pulled at his hair and howled a torturous scream up to the night sky like a hysterical werewolf. He couldn't believe he'd fallen victim to such a scoundrel. *Again.* He huffed his way to his car, his naked body shivering in the wind, carrying Dwight's victory inside him all the way home.

# CHAPTER 5

*One week later*

Ripped.

Torn.

Not whole.

Will heal, but never as it was before.

This was Levi's own prognosis for his battered behind and crushed ego. Neither would be the same again. How could he stay the same person after such a bitter betrayal? He couldn't. He had lost parts of himself he would never be able to recover.

It had been bad enough Dwight tying him up and letting Blondie have his way with him but what added salt to his wounds was how he'd stupidly gone to Dwight's later that evening to be a victim all over again.

*What the fuck was I thinking?*

Levi hadn't been thinking. That was the problem. He knew now he was probably still in a state of shock at the time, too numb from what had happened when tied to his bed to be able to think straight. The sight of Dwight standing in his doorway shirtless, oozing masculine sex appeal, had been too much for Levi's mushy mind to take. Rather than give Dwight the abusive burst he deserved, Levi had succumbed to the intense attraction he felt for a man who was much more dangerous than he ever realised. The sex they shared was electric, off the charts, dick-achingly amazing, but like most enjoyable things in this world it was bad for his health.

Dwight and his bareback sidekick had done more than damage his arsehole, they'd totally fucked-up the image of who Levi thought he was. For years now, Levi had viewed himself as a young guy who was in control, someone whose mere presence demanded respect, an alpha among his peers. He didn't feel like he was much of an alpha of anything anymore. He'd opened his heart and soul to the dangers of vulnerability and had been burned beyond repair.

He reached down under the blanket and scraped a finger along his degraded orifice, remembering how it felt to be filled with liquid shame, being treated as nothing more than something to cum in. Dwight had made sure Levi felt exactly like what had been written on his back. A cum bucket.

He'd never thought of himself as submissive but Dwight had a way to make him crave submission, make him want nothing more than to be a *daddy's boy*. Not anymore. From now on Levi was adamant he would regain control and be the alpha male he was born to be. Heaven help the next man who found his way to Levi's cock because they would be getting treated like absolute trash.

Glancing at the time on his bedside clock, Levi groaned when he saw it was nearly eleven a.m. He had promised Josh he would swing by his place after lunch so they could hang out and catch up. He didn't want to go but he'd been putting off meeting up ever since Josh had untied him and Levi knew he couldn't avoid his best friend any longer. In fact, Levi had avoided everyone and everything for the past week. He hadn't ventured farther than the dairy down the road, skipping a whole week of classes and had refused to answer his phone until last night when Josh had called. Peach had rung multiple times earlier in the week, probably wondering when they would be catching up for lunch, but Levi was too depressed to face the world.

*But today I get back to it.*

He'd allowed himself the week to wallow in misery and self-pity but today he would make a point of getting back out there. It didn't matter if his smile was real or not, it would be on his face regardless. There were parties to attend, songs to dance to and people to fuck. Candy Boy might have been down but was by no means out.

Casting his blanket aside, Levi rolled out of bed and got to his feet. He pulled on a fresh pair of tightie-whities, pushing his piss-hard cock to the side, and made his way to his en suite to relieve his bladder. Once his morning wood had softened some, his dick erupted like a cannon, his piss splashing loudly into the water below. Levi shook his dick free of dribbles then walked back into his room to check himself out in the mirror.

He surveyed his neck, making sure all the lovebites Dwight had given him had gone. They had faded away two days ago but he was constantly paranoid they might reappear or that he'd missed spotting one. The hickeys may have healed but he still felt dirty in ways that couldn't be seen. Dwight had left a stain on his soul that could only be removed through revenge. And Levi knew he would get his revenge…he just wasn't sure when or how.

Levi had to right this wrong. Men like Dwight Stephenson—*povo pieces of shit*—weren't entitled to have the last laugh. That wasn't the way the world worked. Dwight needed to be reminded he was beneath Levi. It didn't matter how Levi had come into money, the fact was he had plenty and Dwight had none.

And Blondie… he too would feel Levi's wraith. Just as soon as Levi found out who the raping fucker was. All he knew was that the guy was blond—*surprise, surprise*—

and that he had the initials DS tattooed on his lower back. That was about the only detail he'd been able to make out from the quick glimpse into the bedroom before Dwight had tackled him to the floor. The only other thing he knew about this Blondie was that the guy brewed cum by the gallon. Levi took a few shuddering breaths, trying to tame the ache of shame swelling inside his chest as he thought about the embarrassing noises his arse had made dispelling the mystery man's semen from his body. Levi had spent the whole week slut-shaming himself for sharing such an intimate moment with a man whose name he didn't even know. It didn't matter if he hadn't explicitly consented to such a personal act, he still felt dirty.

Levi jumped when his reflection was joined by that of his stepfather standing behind him. He spun around, clutching his chest. "Could you try bloody knocking next time." He exhaled slowly, calming down from his fright. "I nearly shit myself."

"Are you sure you didn't? Because this room smells a lot like someone took a dump in here." Mark's judgemental gaze flicked around Levi's messy room.

"If you're looking for the stand-up comedy bar then you have the wrong place."

"Somebody's feeling a bit titchy today." Mark grinned. "Come to think of it, you've been pretty titchy with me the past week. Have I done something I don't know about?"

*Yes. Your sweaty briefs.*

"I'm always titchy when you're around," Levi said. He turned back to face the mirror again, and began to mindlessly style his hair so he could avoid making direct eye contact with his stepfather.

Mark just stood there with his hands on his hips, a gormless stare on his stupid mug as he watched Levi piss about with his hair. Levi's stepfather was blissfully unaware of the fucked-up relationship he and Levi now shared but Levi knew. He had done his best to avoid Mark all week, not wanting to lay eyes on the man whose whiffy gruts he'd sniffed under the illusion that the musky stench of ball sweat belonged to Dwight.

"Can I help you?" Levi glared in the mirror at his stepfather's reflection.

"You can actually. Your mother and I were just talking outside with the new neighbour and we've invited him over for coffee so I thought it would be a good idea for you to come down and introduce yourself as well." Mark paused, an almost dreamy look in his eye. "He seems a great guy. It will be good to make a new friend who lives nearby. Since Daryl moved his family back to Auckland I haven't had anyone in the neighbourhood I can just invite over for a quiet drink on a week night."

"Who's the new neighbour?"

"If you come down and introduce yourself then you can find out."

Levi sighed internally, not in the mood for his stepfather's sass. "Can you at least tell me what house they have moved into?"

"Mrs Anderson's home."

"Did she sell it?"

"Edith died three months ago, Levi."

"Oh… what did she die of?"

"Lack of breath."

"Har, har," Levi groaned.

"Did you seriously not know Edith had passed away?"

"Do I sound like I know she died?"

"How unobservant can you be?" Mark shook his head. "Her family were renovating the place for weeks after her funeral. All *eight* of her children. There were so many of them they made the street look like a bloody car yard."

"Come to think of it, I do remember you complaining about the cars."

"Bloody Catholics and their large families," Mark moaned.

"I thought you were Catholic."

"No," Mark said firmly. "I'm Anglican."

"Aren't they the same thing?"

Mark snorted. "Try telling that to the people who died during the reformation."

"Sorry I'm not as old as you to be around when all of history happened."

"I'm forty-five," Mark sighed. "Not a million."

"Are you sure? 'Cos I think you look closer to the million mark… Mark."

"You can say what you like about my age but you can't bring me down because I know I am looking really good at the moment. I've lost ten kilos since I started jogging and using the home gym again." He lifted his shirt up nearly to his neck, rubbing a hand over his midriff and stomach. "See… my tummy's mostly gone."

Levi's nose picked up the imaginary scent of musky ball sweat from the sight of his stepfather's hairy torso in the mirror. "Put it away, Tilikum."

Mark chuckled, dropping his shirt back down. "You know, I'm thinking if I keep this up I might get my abs back."

"As if you ever had abs."

"I did too. I had a great body in my twenties. I was very popular with the ladies."

"Yeah, so you could breastfeed their babies with your man boobs."

Mark gaped, he didn't seem to know if he should laugh or be angry. "Before you attempt to ruin my self-esteem any further, I better tell you that I need you to pick Danny up for me today, please."

"Why can't you pick him up. He's your son."

"I would pick him up but your mother and I are going to Alan and Sue's for a barbeque," Mark said, pausing to sigh. "I would have rather stayed home, you know how I hate barbeque dinners, but I have to go because Alan has invited one of his architect friends especially just so they can talk with me about ideas for the latest property development I'm working on. I wouldn't mind but I already have an architect firm I deal with for my developments and I sort of feel like Alan is taking advantage of the situation because…"

Levi zoned out, Mark's voice just becoming white noise as he rambled on and on about pointless bullshit Levi had no interest in. "If I agree to pick Danny up will you please stop talking."

Mark stopped talking and nodded.

"So when and where do I have to pick dipshit up?" Levi asked, still playing with his hair in the mirror.

"Your brother is not a dipshit."

"He's not my brother."

"You don't have to share the same blood as someone to be family."

"Yeah, yeah," Levi sighed. "Just tell me when and where to pick Danny up from."

"Five o'clock from Kaleb's house."

Levi groaned. "I don't know why Danny insists on hanging out with that fuck face."

"Language," Mark grumbled before adding, "but I must say I agree with you for once. I'm not sure Kaleb is Danny's friend for the right reasons."

"That's what I keep telling Danny. Kaleb is just a user."

Levi didn't bother responding and the talking dried up. Levi hoped Mark would take the silence as his que to leave the room but his stepfather just stood there, gawking at Levi styling his hair.

"You can go now," Levi said bluntly.

"Gee, thank you for giving me permission on leaving a room in my own house."

"I don't mean to be rude but you keep standing there staring at me and it's getting sort of creepy now."

"I've been standing here having a conversation with you Levi. It's what adults do."

"Really? They like to stand and check out their stepson in just his underwear for five minutes?"

"What on earth are you insinuating?"

"For you to stop being a homo and let me get dressed in private."

"You know, Levi, I had hoped you would have grown out of your teenage tantrums by now. Danny's three years younger than you and he doesn't behave like this."

"That's because Danny's too young to throw teenage tantrums. He still hasn't gone through puberty yet."

"Don't be so stupid."

"His voice still cracks on a good day."

"Danny's voice stopped cracking years ago." Mark's face twitched. "Well… it stopped at least a year ago."

Poor Danny had probably suffered the squeakiest voice change in history. From the age of thirteen to just the end of last year, Danny's slowly deepening voice would switch gears loudly and frequently, going from regular teen mode one moment then suddenly ricocheting to a high-pitched stratosphere the next. His voice had found its home now, and like the rest of Danny it strongly resembled his father, a moderately masculine depth with a touch of warmth.

Levi had always tried not to make too fun of Danny for it, he didn't like to make fun of people for things that were perfectly natural. A lesson he'd been taught at thirteen when busted doing something completely natural himself. But that didn't mean he wasn't above mocking Danny in front of Mark. Mocking Danny always pissed Mark off, and anything that pushed his snobby stepfather's buttons was fine in Levi's books.

"Nope. I think it's pretty safe to say Danny's still waiting for his vagina to drop." Levi couldn't resist getting another dig in.

"You really are a heartless little shit at time," Mark said heatedly.

"Calm your farm. It was just a joke."

"Danny idolises you but all you ever do is pick him to pieces."

"I only do it when you're around. Not to his face."

"And that makes it okay, does it?" Mark shook his head and muttered, "Sometimes I wonder where I went wrong with you."

"Chill out, Mark. You're not the one who went wrong with me." Levi paused to pout at himself in the mirror. "Barry fucked me up long before you ever came along."

A genuine look of concern flashed across Mark's face. "What did he do?"

"Nothing," Levi lied. "It was just a vain attempt at another joke."

"Hmm." Mark seemed to relax, finally making his way out of Levi's bedroom. "Remember to come say hi to our new neighbour when you're finished dropping your vagina in the mirror."

Levi bit the tail end of a laugh. "Dick."

With Mark gone, Levi finally left the safety of the mirror and went and sat at his desk and opened his laptop.

After spending most of the week too depressed to do much more than sleep or smoke like a chimney, Levi had stayed up late the night before writing about what had happened to him, covering every dirty detail in unflinching honesty about how he'd been tied up, gagged with his stepfather's underwear, fucked brutally by *Daddy* and then fucked raw by a complete stranger. He didn't just describe the physical activities, he went into great detail about how it had fucked with his head and the shame he felt at being used.

In some ways writing what had happened to him had been therapeutic but nowhere near enough to completely remove the shame he still felt from the incident. When he'd finished writing the story, which he named Taken Candy, he very nearly deleted the whole document, unsure about sharing with the world what had happened to him. But in the end he decided to post the story for two reasons. Firstly, he didn't see the point in not milking the story for some cash. A story that raunchy was bound to increase Candy Boy's income, and why not make some money from his sexual suffering. Secondly, he hoped it might help him discover who Blondie was. It was unlikely but he had left a note at the bottom of the story asking if any of his followers living in New Zealand knew of anyone with a *DS* tattoo. Yep, an absolute fucking long shot but it was the best shot he had at finding out Blondie's identity.

Levi logged into his blog account and discovered about a dozen messages waiting for him. The first message was from a concerned follower encouraging him to go to the police and report what had happened to him.

**You really should go to the police and report what happened. No one should have to go through what you did. I hope you're okay Candy Boy. xx**

"If only you knew me," Levi said dryly to himself. His dark personal observation didn't stem from self-hatred but common sense. While this follower had a kind heart, Levi knew some people online might think he deserved what had happened to him. After all, Candy Boy wasn't renowned for treating his hook ups kindly. The very next message he opened up confirmed this.

**About time a nasty prick like you got a taste of his own medicine. I hope it fucking hurt!**

"It sure did, fuckface." Levi resisted the urge to respond with a hateful message. Everyone on the Crashing Hearts site received abuse from time to time but Levi tended to get more than his fair share of hate because of how honest he was about sex and the people he screwed. If someone he'd fooled round with wasn't overly hot then he would say so, if they were useless at sucking dick then he would share that too. No one was above criticism from Candy Boy, not even Levi himself.

The rest of his emails were horny one liners from men who looked like they'd typed with one hand, telling him how much cum they'd blown from reading his story. The final message in his inbox was from Demon Dave. Levi didn't usually take much notice of who emailed him but Demon Dave was an exception. He had been following Candy Boy for over three years and often sent emails congratulating Levi on his conquests.

**I must say how much I have enjoyed your last two stories Candy Boy. I know you must be reeling from being turned out in such brutal fashion but I hope you find some solace in learning more about yourself from what happened. My only disappointment with these latest blog entries is you**

have not included pictures. I would have loved to see a picture of Blondie's seed leaking out of you.

**PS I have never met anyone with the initials DS tattooed on their body but I have faith you will find this Blondie. After all, Fitzroy is only so big.**

Levi flinched when he read that last line. "How the fuck do you know where I live?"

Aside from his profile saying he lived in New Zealand, Levi gave very little away about his identity and location. Before he deleted his account in fear of yet another person finding out he was the mastermind behind Candy Boy, Levi calmed himself down when he realised who Demon Dave was.

He laughed at himself for not working it out sooner. *Dwight, you fucking prick.* That's who it had to be. Dwight had told him the first night they fucked how he was a big fan of Candy Boy's stories, so he must have had his own Crashing Hearts account. Levi drummed his fingers on the desk, wondering what to write back. As much as he wanted to send an essay long piece of abuse, Levi kept the message short and relatively calm.

**I know this is you Dwight so stop playing games and just tell me who Blondie is. I have a right to know.**

Levi clicked send and shut down his laptop. His balls began to make their presence known, aching and throbbing with the pain of lustful need. If he knew it wouldn't hurt so much then he would have punched himself in the nuts to make them stop. It seemed that even after everything Dwight had done, Levi could not switch off the intense attraction he felt for a man who could dish out as much desire as he could pain. It irritated him no end knowing that the best sex of his life had been with such a scoundrel, a brutish man who was old enough to be his father. A man strong enough to be his *Daddy*.

"What the fuck is wrong with me?" Levi groaned down at his hardening dick.

*Plenty*, was his mind's response.

# CHAPTER 6

Levi spent ages trying to deice what to wear, fossicking
through his clothes until he settled on a clean pair of khakis
and a yellow t-shirt with a small picture of four leaf clover
on the front. He rarely wore this t-shirt but a superstitious
part of him was hoping it might act like a good luck charm
and help his visit with Josh go smoothly.

Once dressed, he crept downstairs, hoping to slip
away unnoticed without having to say hello to the new
neighbour, but just as Levi got to the bottom of the stairs
he walked straight into the path of his mother coming
down the hallway.

"Are you coming to say hello to Ameesh?" his
mother asked.

"Is that the new neighbour?" Levi asked.

"Yes. He seems quite nice." She nodded then
casually added. "He's invited me and Mark over to have
dinner with him and Martin next week."

"Who's Martin?"

"Ameesh's partner."

"They're gay?"

"Yes, darling."

Levi sniggered.

"Don't laugh," his mother scolded. "You know
better than to make fun of someone's sexuality."

"It's not that," Levi said, wiping the grin off his
face. "It's knowing Mark is in there entertaining his new

gay bestie. He came upstairs before going on about how great it would be to have a close friend who lives nearby he can have over for drinks."

His mother giggled. "Yes, I think your stepfather got quite the shock when Ameesh just told us that his partner was called Martin."

"I wish I could have seen his face."

"I don't think Ameesh noticed but I did see a small crack in Mark's smile when he heard that titbit of information." She chuckled lightly. "Mark is a bit funny about things like that."

"Yeah, because he's a homophobe."

"I wouldn't say that."

"I would. Remember him being up in arms about gay marriage becoming legal?"

"I don't think Mark is anti-anyone, he's just a bit"—she nibbled her lip—"old-fashioned."

"You mean he's a dick."

"Be nice, darling." She smiled with her eyes. "Now come and say hello to Ameesh."

Levi rubbed his neck. "I would but I have to go see Josh. He's expecting me soon."

"Just come in and say a quick hello. You don't have to stay for long. I've been telling Ameesh all about my wonderful son so it would be nice for him to meet you."

"He might think you're a liar once he meets me." Levi smirked.

She laughed. "Don't be silly. Everybody who meets you thinks you're wonderful."

Levi looked down at spotted a piece of paper in his mother's hand. "What's that?"

"Oh. It's one of the missing posters of Shay I had made for Connie." She held it up and showed Levi the picture.

Beneath the bold heading of ***MISSING. PLEASE HELP*** was a photo of Shay Jacobs. The picture was in colour which made perfect sense because it was only in colour that you could truly appreciate Shay's most striking feature. His eyes. The missing man had the bluest eyes Levi had ever seen on a person but what made them even more captivating was the contrast to his light-brown skin. With a blonde, European mother and a dark-skinned, Maori father, Shay had hit the genetic jackpot. The striking contrast helped add beauty and an endless supply of female admirers to a young man with otherwise average looks. What had also helped Shay become the most well-laid guy in Brixton was his personality. He had always been a bad boy with a heart of gold, doing a tonne of stupid shit that seemed to impress women looking to experience the love of a bad boy who wouldn't beat the shit out of them when he got drunk. Unfortunately Shay's heart of gold had become poisoned with a meth addiction that saw him pulling more and more criminal stunts in a bid to feed his habit and drug debt. A debt that was most likely the reason he had been missing for close to two months.

"Such a handsome boy," Levi's mother cooed. "I do hope he's alright."

Levi didn't even say anything but the look on his face told his mother what he thought.

"I know you think he is most likely... gone, but I have been praying we find him safe and well for Connie's sake."

Levi's mother was a big believer in the power of prayer, insisting God had answered her many times before. Levi never liked hearing this. Not because he doubted the possibility of there being a God but because of the terrifying consequences awaiting him if there was one.

"You know that it would be better if you just post on Facebook how he is missing, right?"

"Of course. Connie has been posting on all social media for weeks now but so far nothing." Levi's mother paused, giving Shay's picture a sad little smile. "Apparently Ameesh is a detective with Fitzroy Police so I am hoping he may be able to help."

"I thought I could smell bacon."

"None of that, please." She swatted his arm, giggling. "Now come introduce yourself and try not to run off straight away, at least stay and talk for two minutes."

He followed his mother to the kitchen, squinting as bright sunlight blinded him through the numerous glass panels that made the room look more like a glasshouse than an actual kitchen. Mark and Ameesh were sat at the table talking away. Levi wasn't surprised to discover that their new neighbour with the name Ameesh was Indian but he was surprised by his accent. It wasn't Kiwi or Indian. He couldn't quite put his finger on Ameesh's accent until he heard Mark ask, "How long has it been since you left South Africa?"

"Martin and I left Durban five years ago. We spent a year in Auckland before moving down here to Fitzroy."

"Ameesh," Levi's mother said in a sunny voice as she sat down at the table. "I want you to meet my son, Levi."

Levi walked towards Ameesh who stood up and stretched out his hand. "Nice to meet you, Levi."

"Same," Levi mumbled, his hand going limp in the shake.

"Wow, you look just like your mum," Ameesh commented.

Levi's mother may have been blonde while Levi was brown-haired but they did share the same attractive face and hazel eyes, their beauty gifting them both the ability to turn heads when they walked into a room.

"Yes, I often tell Levi how much he looks like a girl," Mark joked.

Ameesh coughed up a laugh, probably out of politeness, Levi thought.

Ameesh sat back down and Levi went and leaned against the island bench and folded his arms, waiting out the two minutes his mother had asked him to.

"Ameesh, I hope you don't mind but I wanted to ask you if you know if the Fitzroy police are looking into a certain missing person case."

"Missing person?" Ameesh frowned. "Who?"

Levi's mother slid over the missing poster. "Shay Jacobs. He's been missing for nearly two months and his mother is worried sick."

Ameesh's lips curved into a slight smile before quickly vanishing. "Ahh, yes. Shay Jacobs."

"You know the case?"

"I'm not familiar with any case about him being missing but we all know Shay and his mother very well down at the station."

That didn't sound good.

Ameesh frowned at Levi's mother. "No offense, Jenny, but I wouldn't have picked a lovely lady like you knowing a family like that."

"Jenny does a lot of charity work in Brixton," Mark quickly said, not wanting to tell his new neighbour he was married to a former Brixton housewife.

Levi's mother didn't care. She was not ashamed of her past. "I do but I also lived in Brixton for fifteen years before I married Mark. Shay and his mother Connie were our next door neighbours and good friends."

"So you would know what Shay is like?" Ameesh replied.

"I know he isn't the best-behaved boy in the world but he is a sweetheart really," Levi's mother said.

"Considering Shay is 26 I would say he is very much a man," Ameesh said flatly. "And not a very nice one."

"You know his age?" Mark quirked an eyebrow. "You must be very familiar with him then."

"We have booked Shay so many times that most of us at the station would know his birth date off by heart and the address of the last ten couches he has been staying on."

While Mark laughed and Levi smirked, Levi's mother remained rigid with a serious expression.

"I know Shay is no angel but isn't it your job to find missing people regardless of their background?" She glared at Ameesh.

Levi smiled, enjoying the suddenly tense atmosphere his mother had created.

Mark stiffened in his chair. "We shouldn't really bother Ameesh about work stuff, honey. It is his weekend as well."

Ameesh ignored Mark and focused on Levi's mother. "I can understand how frustrating this must be for Connie but has she told you this isn't the first time Shay has gone *missing?*" He used dramatic air quotes, speaking in a tone that straddled both friendly and mocking.

"Shay has never gone missing for this long though," Levi's mother hurled back. "Two months is a long time to not contact anyone."

"I am sure Shay will come home when he is finished doing whatever he is doing," Ameesh said.

Something about the way he said it felt rehearsed and phony as fuck, Levi thought.

Levi's mother must have thought the same thing. "I'm sorry for coming at you so strongly about this. I do apologise. But do you really believe he will come home if he has been missing for this long?"

"Are you asking me to answer that as a detective or as a guest in your house," Ameesh asked.

"Whichever is the most honest," she said firmly. "And if you are worried about me telling Connie what you say then you shouldn't worry about that. I lived in Brixton long enough to know how to keep things to myself."

That got a chuckle out of Ameesh. He turned to Mark and said, "Your wife is tougher than she looks."

"Jenny is full of surprises. She is the most amazing and beautiful woman I know." Mark looked adoringly at his wife.

Levi cringed on his stepfather's behalf. The guy was a fucking putz.

Levi's mother ignored the compliment. "Am I wasting my time with these posters?" She waved the piece of paper in the air. "I don't want to keep killing trees if I shouldn't be."

Ameesh chewed his lip in concentration and drummed his long fingers on the table. "This is my personal opinion, nothing official, but let's just say with the kind of money Shay owed to certain people I don't think he will be home for Christmas."

Levi's stomach kicked. When his mother first mentioned Shay had gone missing, Levi had assumed the Brixton rebel was dead but hearing a detective say it made it feel more real and final somehow.

"Thank you, Ameesh." Levi's mother gave their guest a dismal smile. "I appreciate your honesty."

"I'm sorry to share such bad news but I suspect you may have thought the worst already."

"It's okay." She shrugged away her sadness. "Let's talk about nicer things."

"Yes, let's," Mark agreed.

"Tell me, Ameesh." Levi's mother smiled at their guest. "How are you finding the neighbourhood? It's lovely out here, isn't it?"

"You're telling me. Martin and I have been wanting to buy a place out here since we moved to Fitzroy. We just love how many trees and parks there are in the area. It feels like living in an urban jungle. And the views out to sea are simply stunning."

"It's fantastic," Mark said. "I wouldn't dream of living anywhere else."

*Yet you tell me to live somewhere else all the fucking time.*

As the chitter chatter continued, Levi discovered that Ameesh's partner Martin was a nurse. He wasn't sure how much the couple's combined salaries would be but he figured the pair of them must have squeezed out every penny they had to buy Mrs Anderson's old place. Shelter Grove was not cheap with an average asking price of close to two million dollars for the privilege of living in Fitzroy's best neighbourhood.

"I'm looking forward to trying out some of the café's down the road," Ameesh commented. "They look really good."

"You and Martin must try out Chaos," said Levi's mother. "It's a new café that we have set up at The Community." When Ameesh frowned, Levi's mother expanded on what she meant by *The Community.*

While Levi's mother explained how the spiritual sanctuary—or cult as Levi often teased—she belonged to had opened a café up in one of their orchards, Levi remained leaned against the bench, taking the opportunity to give Ameesh a visual appraisal. The smartly dressed thirty-something had an air of confidence about him that usually came when you had money, and anyone who lived on this street had plenty of that. A tidy, short beard covered his square jaw, adding an element of gruffness to his otherwise friendly face. He looked fit enough to chase criminals but his tummy prodded the bottom of his shirt just enough to give away the beginning of a paunch.

The longer Levi stared the more annoyed he got that Ameesh didn't slip him a sly glance of some kind to show his appreciation of Levi's beauty. *Stare at me fucker. Gay guys usually do.* But Ameesh didn't look Levi's way once, too busy giving Levi's mother his undivided attention. *Maybe he's too worried Mum and Mark will notice.* Levi wondered if that was it but his ego didn't believe that was a good enough excuse. He considered himself hot enough for people to risk staring at him no matter how awkward or inconvenient the moment might be.

Then Ameesh did. Very briefly but it was definitely a sly glance Levi's way.

*That's more fucking like it.*

Levi rewarded Ameesh's bravery by slipping a hand under his shirt and scratching his navel, keeping his shirt lifted so his stomach remained on show.

As expected, Ameesh shot him another glance, this time for longer, his dark brown eyes burning into the strip of skin Levi was teasing him with. Levi's mother and Mark didn't notice, allowing Ameesh to stare a third time, this time dropping his gaze to Levi's crotch.

*That's right. You wish you could suck this dick.*

Levi pretended not to notice Ameesh checking him out, continuing to casually stroke the hairs below his bellybutton and letting the detective's eyes feast on him. Once Levi grew tired of having his ego stroked by Ameesh's burning eyes, he interjected the conversation and told everyone he had to get going. He was nearly out the front door when hurried footfall sounded behind him. For a brief moment, he worried he'd flirted too much and had the new neighbour running after him but when he spun around he saw it was his mother.

"Before you go," she said, coming to a stop right in front of him. "I was wondering if you could do me a favour?"

"What kind of favour?"

"I wanted to ask if you could please drive to Brixton and see if anybody knows anything about where Shay might be." She sighed. "I wouldn't ask but as you saw in the kitchen the Fitzroy police have no interest in doing their job."

"You heard what Ameesh said, Shay's probably dead."

"He may well be but someone needs to find out for sure."

"How am I suppose to find out? I can't rock into Brixton pretending I'm Mr Plod."

"You could visit some of Shay's friends. See if they know anything."

"Wouldn't have Connie already done that?"

"Yes but you know as well as I do that the people who might know anything won't tell Connie where Shay might be."

Levi's mother wasn't wrong. Brixton's shadier residents lacked all sorts of morals but the one thing they didn't do was nark.

"But I'm not friends with Shay's friends anymore," Levi whined, really not wanting to pay house visits in his old neighbourhood. He'd stopped making house calls after the horrific balls-up that had been his Twisted Candy story.

His mother tilted her head. "You know Scott, don't you?"

"Barely."

"But you know him well enough to ask him if he knows anything about where Shay might be?"

Levi hadn't seen Scott Morris for over a year but the sometimes drug dealer would probably talk if he was

63

stoned or drunk—which he most likely would be—and if he didn't talk then a fifty-dollar note would make him open his trap.

"I just want to get Connie some closure." Her voice quavered. "I fear for the worst but we need some sort of confirmation."

"Why though? Connie wasn't a good friend to you even when we lived there. You know her and Dad used to—"

"I know very well what Connie and your father got up to but this isn't just for Connie's sake; it is for Shay's." She stared at him sternly and lowered her voice. "I think you and I owe Shay that much at least. If it wasn't for him then we would not have the wonderful life we do now."

Levi gulped. His mother never talked about that. Never! It was an unspoken rule that neither of them bring up the fateful night eight years earlier that resulted in the bloodstained shirt hanging in Levi's closet. A night that resulted in a lifetime of lies about how his father never came home from "going out to buy a packet of cigarettes."

"Please, darling, can you just see if anyone knows anything. Anything at all."

"Okay, Mum," Levi whispered. "I'll see what I can do."

# CHAPTER 7

Levi was a ball of nerves as he drove along the highway towards his best mate's place. It seemed stupid to feel so anxious about visiting someone he knew so well but that was what made coming here difficult. Josh, his best friend for ten years, had seen him in a way Levi had never intended him to see him—tied face down to a bed with his arse a reservoir of seed.

Josh may have reacted well at the time, incredibly well even, but it didn't change the fact the dynamic of their friendship was bound to change. The blowjob Levi had given Josh for his birthday was one thing but he'd always hoped to play the bi-curious card, maybe convince Josh to play the card himself, but that was not an option now. Dwight had left Levi's body so corrupted there was nothing curious about it. And now Josh knew.

This pissed Levi off in more way than one. For starters, it meant any chance of coercing Josh into letting him suck him off again was highly unlikely—which was probably Dwight's intention—but even more annoying was the way it felt like Josh had something over him now. A dubious piece of scandal that would always be available to the dark-blond stud if he chose to use it. Not that Josh ever would, he wasn't like that. Josh was one of the good guys but that didn't mean he was immune to making snide comments under the guise of playful banter when they were alone. It was those digs Levi wasn't looking forward to.

Levi indicated to change lanes, taking the off ramp to Glen Avon, an inner-city suburb packed with students and young professionals who paid through the nose for the pretentious honour of living stumbling distance to town. This was a suburb Peach liked to call "Flyer Central" on account of how many of Fitzroy's young and wealthy lived here. Most parties Levi attended were around here, lush pads decked out with indulgence.

Josh lived in a sunny two-bedroom bungalow on one of Glen Avon's pretty tree-lined streets, the type of property that should have been way out of Josh's price range but luckily for Josh the house was owned by Levi's stepfather who rented it to Josh at a ridiculously cheap rate. Josh's good fortune didn't stem from the fact Mark had a soft spot for the sensible and hardworking Josh—which he did—but because when it had been offered Mark thought it meant Levi would be keen to move out and go flatting with his best friend. This was one of just many examples that proved Mark was a fucking idiot. Why pay reduced rent to live in a crappy old bungalow when you can live in a mansion for free? When presented with the option of moving into the gentrified bungalow, Levi swiftly turned it down, much to his stepfather's horror.

Mark hadn't been the only one disappointed at Levi's refusal to leave the nest, so had Josh. Levi's best mate tried for weeks to convince him to move in, insisting how much fun it would be living together.

"Go on, man. Don't you think it would be awesome the two of us sharing a pad together? Think of all the fun we can get up to," Josh had said.

"It probably would be but it's also fun living in a ten-bedroom house with a housekeeper I don't have to pay to clean up all my shit," was Levi's reply at the time.

"If you're worried about us living in a mess then don't worry. I'm pretty good at being tidy."

"Honestly, Josh, I'm a messy pig."

"Lucky for you you're my best friend so I don't mind cleaning up after you… sometimes."

"Unless you fancy picking up rubbers filled with my spunk I leave lying around, I don't think you want to clean up after me."

That had put a grimace on Josh's handsome face and put an end to his pleading.

Rather than turn Mark's generous offer down, Josh signed the tenancy without Levi and invited their old friend from high school, Ethan Drinkwater, to move into the second bedroom. Ethan was a nice enough person but he was the very definition of average, Levi thought. The guy was average height, average build, and had very average mousy brown hair atop of his averagely-attractive face. He was neither overly loud or awkwardly shy, just a regular dude who liked his sport, nights out, and chasing girls.

As Levi pulled up outside Josh's house, he could feel the panic rising in him, hands sweating as he approached the front door. He took a quick inhale like he was about to go under water, ready to greet Josh with his *ain't-nothing-wrong* face. Levi was a master of this face; he'd had to use it throughout his life many times, never failing at coming across cool, calm and collected. It was probably one of the few things he had his father to thank for. Without all the shit Barry Buttwell had put Levi and his mother through then he was sure he'd not have the thick skin he had today.

Stepping inside, Levi's nostrils were immediately hit with a light lemon spritz. He discovered the source of the smell as he strolled through the kitchen, the table and benches gleaming with a freshly-cleaned shine. Josh hadn't been lying when he claimed to be a tidy housemate.

"Josh," Levi called out when he found the tidy lounge with no signs of life.

"In my room," Josh called out.

Levi followed the sound of his best mate's voice down the hallway to his bedroom where he found Josh on the floor in the middle of a sit-up routine, his white-socked feet hooked under the end of his bed.

"Sixty-one, sixty-two, sixty-three—won't be long, man—sixty-four, sixty-five, sixty-six..."

Levi stood and watched as a shirtless Josh powered his way towards a hundred sit-ups. His lower half was casually clad in a pair of baggy grey sweatpants as he powered his way towards eighty sit-ups. He looked dreamy the way his tanned chest glistened with sweat, the hair under his arms soaked with perspiration. The longer Levi watched his best mate building up a sweat, the more he could feel his dick coming to life, threatening to tentpole the crotch of his jeans.

*Stay the fuck down.*

The last thing he needed was for Josh to catch him springing an erection. Still, he was almost grateful for the ill-timed arousal since it was the first time he'd felt remotely horny since Dwight and Blondie had fucked him.

Josh unhooked his feet and knee-walked across the floor to grab a towel hanging from the knob on his closet door. He rubbed his face and chest dry then dropped the towel to the floor before chucking a singlet on. "It's good to see you, man. I wasn't sure if you'd come or not."

"Why wouldn't I come?"

"Well, I've barely seen you since... I thought maybe you were avoiding me."

"Sorry about the lack of contact, I've just been really busy with tech the past week." Levi nodded as if that would make his lie more believable. "We have a crazy amount of assignments due at the moment."

Josh eyed him suspiciously but didn't question him. "That's good. Not so much all the assignments but it's good to know you're not avoiding me."

Levi didn't want last week brought up so he changed the topic. "So what's this favour you wanted to ask me?"

Josh got to his feet and sat down on the edge of his bed. "I'm going on holiday for a few weeks and I was wondering if you could feed Phoebe while I am away?"

Phoebe was the world's snobbiest tortoise shell cat but she was Josh's pride and joy. He'd owned her since he was fourteen and when he moved out of his mother's house it was a given that Phoebe would come with him. He treated the cat like she was a queen, feeding her specially bought hearts and livers from the butchers shop down the road.

"Won't Ethan be here to feed her, though?"

"Ethan's in France visiting his sister who just had the baby."

"Oh, that's right. How could I forget." Levi rolled his eyes. Ethan hadn't shut up the past six months about how excited he was to become an uncle. "Maybe he will stop going on and on about it when he gets back. The way he went on you'd think his sister was the first woman to ever have a baby."

Josh sniggered. "You really aren't a baby person are you?"

"Guilty as charged."

"But the question is are you a pussy person?" Josh grinned then quickly added, "You know, keen to look after Phoebe? If you're too busy then I can get Mum to feed her. No biggy."

Levi shook his head. "It's not a problem. I don't mind." Actually he did mind but because it was Josh he would swallow his reluctance and sign up to being Phoebe's slave.

"Thanks, man. I'll make sure she has food in the fridge but I'll make sure to leave money on the kitchen bench so you can get her some more liver from the butcher shop."

Levi nodded. "So where are you going away to? It's not like you to take a holiday."

Josh's face lit with a smile. "I know, right? Work have been begging me for months to take some time off because I have so much accrued holiday pay but I just kept turning it down until Dad turned up here last weekend with a surprise birthday present."

"A surprise birthday present? I thought your present from him was a lopsided space cake," Levi muttered sarcastically.

"That's what I thought but he turned up here last weekend and gave me this." As if electrocuted, Josh shot to his feet and walked over to his nightstand, rummaging through the lower drawer until his hand fished out a white ticket. He walked over to Levi and showed him the ticket.

Levi studied the ticket carefully, reading the print written on it. "Business class seats to Bali!" he blurted.

"Yep. Three whole weeks staying at a five star hotel." Josh grinned excitedly, fanning his face with the ticket. "Can you believe it?"

Levi couldn't believe it. Dwight mowed lawns for a living. How the fuck could he afford to fly business class and stay in luxury accommodation for three weeks. Rather than voice his true thoughts he just mumbled, "That can't be cheap."

"I think it's cost him a fair whack but Dad said he's been saving up and wanted me to have a big gift for my twenty-first."

"If that's the case why didn't he give you the ticket on your actual birthday?" Levi knew in his bones that there was something dodgy about this gift.

"I don't know but I'm just super stoked he's given it to me now. I can't wait to go."

Levi wanted to pick holes with Dwight's gift but he didn't want to rain on Josh's parade. "When do youse go?"

"Dad's already up in Auckland and I meet him up there tomorrow so we can fly out in the evening."

"Tomorrow!" Levi squawked like he'd been shot.

"Yeah, man. One more sleep and then I am on a plane to go suntan in paradise."

"Don't try smuggling drugs in your boogie board."

"Huh?" Josh frowned, unaware of the joke.

"Nothing." Levi smiled. "I hope you have lots of fun."

"I intend to." Josh put the ticket back away then led the way to the lounge so they could sit down and talk some more. Levi purposely chose to sit on the armchair farthest away from the couch where Josh was sitting. His distance did not go unnoticed.

"Could you sit any further away?" Josh lifted an arm and sniffed his pit. "Do I stink that badly?"

Levi faked a laugh. "Yeah, man. You're a reeky bitch." That wasn't true. Josh didn't stink at all, he was such a good guy that even his sweat smelled pleasant.

A smile pulled at Josh's lips. "Anyway, what have you been up to since my birthday?" Levi appreciated that Josh worded the question like he'd never stumbled in on him tied naked to the bed.

*I got punched over by fuckwit Lucas Maxwell, fucked by your dad and then fucked bare by one of your dad's friends before going to see your dad so he could add his load.* "Nothing much. Just chilling at home and studying pretty much."

71

"You must be hitting the books hard because you didn't go to Sadie's party last Saturday. I thought I'd see you there."

Sadie Cunningham was the queen of parties. She didn't need a birthday or engagement to find an excuse to have a good time. At least once a month she would demand her parents go away for the weekend so she could use their house to throw an extravagant bash that would leave the place drenched with spilt liquor and the bathroom laced with illegal substances. Everyone had a good time at a Sadie Cunningham party, especially Levi, but he'd been too low after what had happened with Dwight to bother going out.

"How was it?" Levi asked. "I'm guessing it was pretty epic."

"It was pretty epic," Josh replied. "Major drama epic."

"What happened?"

"Oh, man, it was a crack up." Josh laughed then started to shake his head. "The house was packed, everyone having a good time then all of a sudden a bunch of Benson Bangers crashed the party and—" Josh's story got lost to sniggering laughter. "Oh, man. It was cringe as fuck."

"I bet it was," Levi agreed. Having a Benson Banger turn up to a party was the kiss of death. If you wanted your party to get a good review in Peach's entertainment column then you knew not to invite anyone who'd come into contact with Wade Benson's cock.

"They stormed into the house like they were marching up parliament steps with a petition," Josh said. "They were on a mission I can tell you that much."

"Who were they?" Levi asked. Wade Benson had shagged so many people it was unlikely they'd all crashed the party.

"There was eight of them. Six girls and two guys; Crystal Thompson, Amy Yandle, Brad Kenny... I'm not sure of the others names. Crystal was pretty much the only one who did the talking though, demanding they be allowed to stay and join in with the fun. She was going on about how it was time to put an end to what she called a 'gross form of social apartheid.'"

Crystal Thompson was a leggy brunette with huge tits and an equally big mouth who had been one of the darlings of the scene until one alcohol-fuelled evening she slept with wannabe rock star, Wade Benson. It was common knowledge around town that Crystal had never gotten over being blacklisted from the in-crowd, constantly complaining to anyone who would listen about how unfair it was. On some level Levi sympathised with her but then Crystal knew as well as everyone else that if you were caught fucking Wade Benson you paid the price. A price that made Cersei Lannister's Walk of Shame look like a stroll in the park.

"And what happened?" Levi inquired.

"It was all pretty tame at first with Sadie asking them politely to leave before too many people noticed them but when Crystal began shouting her speech at the top of her lungs then everyone noticed them. People came running in from outside to see what the hell was going on."

"Oh fuck... Sadie must have felt like dying."

"You could say that. I think she was almost in tears when they refused to go."

"What did Peach do?"

"Peach wasn't at the party," Josh said. "I was surprised."

Levi was surprised too. It wasn't like Peach to miss a party. She had to cover it for her work. "She must have sent someone else from the paper to cover it," Levi suggested.

73

"Maybe."

"Back to the banger bitches," Levi said excitedly. "Did Sadie give up and let them stay?"

"Nope. When Sadie's boyfriend saw how upset she was, him and his mates started chanting 'BANGERS, BANGERS, BANGERS' and pretty soon the whole party was chanting it, some people began throwing their drinks over them... some even spat. It got pretty nasty." Josh exhaled, shaking his head. "So after five minutes of being screamed at and getting drenched with drinks and snotty spit, the bangers left the building."

"Holy fuck," Levi whispered.

"Holy fuck indeed." Josh lifted his feet up and tucked them onto the couch, making himself comfortable. "Me and Jessica nearly left it was that uncomfortable."

"How are things with Jessica? Are you two back together?"

"Um, we're sort of back together..."

"Sort of?" When Josh failed to respond, Levi smiled. "Is this the kind of sort of that involves fucking without officially dating?" He laughed.

"It might do." Josh cringed. "I feel bad but I don't know if I wanna get back together, you know? But I—"

"But you like getting laid too much to tell her," Levi interrupted.

Josh nodded, blushing. "Does that make me an arsehole? I always swore I'd never do that to a girl but I just... just like getting laid." Josh's face was riddled with guilt. It was obvious he really didn't like being *that* guy.

Levi chuckled. "Chill out, man. You wouldn't be the first guy in the world to lead a chick on."

"I know but I just feel guilty as. Jessica keeps asking if we're back together and I just keep saying I'm not sure." He chewed his bottom lip. "I'm so glad Dad shouted me this holiday so I can avoid the question for a few weeks but I know she will expect an answer when I get back."

"Why don't you tell her you're not getting back together before you leave then you can have three weeks away to relax and avoid running into her."

"I would but I…"

Levi rolled his eyes. "You've invited her over to stay tonight, haven't you?"

"Got it in one." Josh pointed a finger gun at him. "I can't believe I'm being such a jerk and thinking with my cock."

"It makes a nice change from you always thinking with your ovary."

"Fuck you." Josh laughed and playfully hurled a cushion at him.

"No thanks. I've been fucked more than enough lately," Levi said playfully, launching the cushion back at his best mate. It was only when the cushion whacked Josh right in the centre of his shocked face that Levi realised what he'd said.

# CHAPTER 8

Levi hadn't wanted Josh to bring up the other day but here he was doing it himself. He suddenly realised he didn't feel uncomfortable about it either, Josh's presence was one that made him feel secure, comforted, and safe. Maybe it wasn't such a bad thing to be open with him.

Josh rested into the back of the couch, grinning at Levi, a flicker of curiosity in his eyes.

"Go on. I can tell you're dying to ask me about it." Levi smiled, letting him know it was okay.

"Are you sure it's okay? I don't want to make you feel awkward or anything."

"It's fine," Levi said. "Provided you don't tell anyone then you can ask what you like."

"Of course, bro. I wouldn't say a word. I haven't told anyone about last week."

"Good." Levi gave him a firm nod. "So what do you want to know?"

"Are you gay or bi?" Josh asked, his tone difficult to read.

"You know how many chicks I've fucked so what do you think?"

"Sorry, I just thought maybe your preferences had changed or something. I hear that can happen with some people."

Josh wasn't entirely wrong about that but he didn't need to know the extent of which Levi had shifted along the Kinsey scale so Levi answered his friend with a purposely vague, "Let's just say I am open to suggestion."

"Open to suggestion," Josh echoed quietly, like he was trying the words out for size. "That's a cool way to describe it."

"I'm a cool guy."

Josh snickered then asked, "What's it feel like?"

"What's what feel like?"

"Having a"—Josh pointed with his eyes down towards his crotch—"inside you."

"It feels like a thousand rainbow butterflies kissing inside your butt."

"That sounds positively delightful," Josh said in a campy voice.

"Bend over and I can show you if you like."

Josh laughed. "No thanks. I'll just take your word for it." His face became serious. "Honestly, though, what does it feel like? Wouldn't it hurt?"

Levi took a deep breath, gathering the courage to be as honest as his online alter ego would be. "It hurts. It feels wrong. It feels right. It feels like a connection. It's almost as if you're being pushed outside of your own body but then it morphs into something else... something that feels good. *Really* fucking good."

"Yeah?"

Levi nodded. "I can't speak for every guy who's been fucked but for me it wasn't so much a physical pleasure as it was a mental pleasure. It was like I was giving away a piece of my humility to give the other guy pleasure... and I don't know why but that just heightened the intimacy of everything. Made me feel closer to him than I could ever imagine."

Josh nodded. "You make the whole experience sound really deep... balls deep."

Levi rolled his eyes.

"Sorry, sorry. I'm just teasing." Josh beamed an apologetic smile before his face went straight. "That honestly sounds really trippy."

"Maybe you should try it some time."

"I don't think it's my thing—no offense." Josh blushed. "I've actually tried sticking a finger up there a couple times when I've been having a wank but it just hurts."

"It might feel better if it was someone else's finger," Levi said, only half-joking.

Josh arched one eyebrow. A tiny gesture that communicated so much. Caution. Challenge. Maybe even a little agitation. "Are you into me?" Josh asked seriously. "Like, do you think I'm hot?"

"If you're worried about me trying to get into your pants then you can chill out. I have no intention of fucking up our friendship."

"Then why did you suck my dick," Josh flung back.

"I don't recall you complaining at the time."

"Nar, man, no complaints. You were way better at it than Jessica."

Levi waggled his eyebrows. "Was I now?"

"Yep. She moaned the whole time and kept scraping me with her teeth." Josh winced. "It hurt so much I had to ask her to stop and I haven't asked her to try again. I was actually wondering if you could give her some pointers."

"You fucking what?"

Josh laughed at Levi's shocked response. "I'm joking, egg."

"I hope so. I can't imagine that being a conversation that would go down too well."

"Not as well as you go down."

Levi snorted. "Somebody's on a roll with the one liners today."

"You still haven't answered my question," Josh said bluntly. "Do you think I'm hot?"

Levi sighed like Josh had asked him for his kidney. "Yes, Josh, I think you're hot."

"Really?" Josh sounded surprised.

"I let you put your dick in my mouth, didn't I?"

"I thought it was just a birthday present."

"It's not like I go around giving all my mates blowjobs for their birthdays."

The way Josh shot him a smug grin was reminiscent of Dwight. Josh looked so much like his father that it was hard for Levi not to feel resentful. *But Josh is a good guy*, Levi reminded himself.

"Maybe you just really love the D?" Josh teased.

"I like your D."

"Aww shucks." Josh covered his face with his hands, pretending to be bashful. "I bet you say that to all the boys."

"Only the sexy ones."

"I had no idea I was sexy as well as hot."

"Don't be a dick. You know you're sexy."

"Sexier than you?" Josh arched one of his perfectly-shaped eyebrows.

*No.* "Yes."

It was obvious Josh was enjoying this. They had always liked to make jokes about who was the better looking between them. They were both hot enough in their own way not to be bothered by the other's beauty.

"Bullshit." Josh laughed. "You're too vain to think that."

"You're right." Levi grinned. "But you are a close second."

"Some might say I am a distant first?"

"Some might be retarded."

They both laughed.

"Does it bother you?" Levi asked. "Me finding you attractive?"

"Not at all. I find it really flattering to be honest."

"Flattering enough to let me suck you off again?"

"I wouldn't go that far," Josh said edgily.

"Are you sure?"

Silence crept in, and unspoken words floated between them. Neither of them looked away.

Josh cleared his throat. "Can I tell you something if you promise not to get the wrong impression?"

"What's the wrong impression?"

"That I am into guys."

"Yeah, man. You can tell me whatever you like. I know you're straight."

Josh twisted a section of his fringe around his finger—a rare nervous gesture. "You know how I said I gave you the last week to give you some space?"

Levi nodded.

"I was also doing that to give myself some space. I needed time to wrap my head around these feelings I had when I found you."

"Feelings?"

"I don't want you to get the wrong idea but…" his words trailed off. "But there was something about the way you looked tied to the bed that was unbelievably hot."

*What. The. Fuck.*

Josh's confession charged the air, shivers skittering along Levi's arms and rousing the tiny hairs on his nape. He began to wonder if the Stephenson men had more in common than just handsome faces and seven-inch dicks. He wiped his mouth, keeping his hazel eyes glued to his best friend.

"I honestly don't know what it was but something about that scene was incredibly sexy," Josh continued.

"You just looked so vulnerable and something about it just spoke to me if that makes sense."

"It makes perfect sense."

"Oh, man. You must be thinking I'm so fucking weird right now." Josh blushed.

"Not at all. It's my turn to be flattered."

"Just to be clear, it's nothing to do with you being a guy."

"I fully know where you're coming from," Levi said. "Sometimes we find ourselves attracted to situations, not necessarily the people."

"Yeah, man. That's it. You got it in one. I found the situation sexy. Not you." Josh smirked. "Sorry. Like, you are sexy… and you looked great naked but you just don't have the parts I go for."

"No worries." Levi really wasn't worried. He didn't care if Josh found him attractive or not, what he cared for was the opportunity he could sense. His best mate had no idea but he'd just reopened a door to something Levi thought had closed forever.

Josh put his feet back on the floor and stretched his long legs. "I wish I could meet a girl who'd let me tie her up and blindfold her with my underwear."

"Who said it has to be a girl?"

Josh arched an eyebrow. "Say what?"

"You said yourself you liked what you saw, why not recreate the scene?"

"You'd seriously do that?"

"I'm not so keen on being tied up again but I don't mind being naked in front of you."

"With my briefs on your face?" The way Josh said it made it obvious that was the part he was interested in.

"If that's what you want?"

Josh blew out a breath. "Oh, man. I think that would be weirder than you sucking my dick."

"Then flop it out and I'll do that instead," Levi teased.

Josh laughed. "I thought you said you wouldn't try getting into my pants."

"Sorry. Sorry. It was a joke. I didn't mean to make you uncomfortable."

"It's fine," Josh said. "Truth be told, I'm not entirely against letting you give me another blowjob."

"You're not?"

"Like I said before, you were good at it. It felt good. I like feeling good."

"Then what's the problem?"

"I don't want to make it a habit. Like, how fucked up would that be for our friendship if I started letting you suck my dick whenever we hung out."

"If you ask me, I think it would do wonders for our friendship."

Josh smirked. "Of course you'd say that—cum bucket."

Levi laughed even though the crude name made his blood boil.

"But the main reason I can't let you suck me is because it would be cheating and you know how I feel about people who cheat."

"I didn't think you and Jessica were back together though?"

"We sort of are, we sort of aren't." Josh dragged a hand through his hair.

"I see," Levi mumbled, his horny hopes dashed. There was no point in arguing. If Josh considered it cheating then it was cheating and Josh would never cheat. Levi slumped back in the chair, dropping his gaze to the floor. *Fucking Jessica.* When Levi peeked back up at Josh, he was surprised to see a soft smile in his eyes.

"I know a blowjob is a big no no but sniffing my underwear isn't technically cheating, is it?"

Levi perked up, grinning. "I don't think so."

"Mates do stupid dares in front of each other all the time, right? So if I were to say 'Levi, I dare you to get naked and sniff my undies,' then that's probably okay."

Levi's pulse quickened, his dick a hot throbbing heartbeat in his pants. "Was that just a suggestion or the first dare?"

Josh hitched an impish eyebrow. "The first dare."

Levi's skin heated as he stood up and unbuttoned his pants, pulling them down just enough to show the hard bulge in his underwear.

"Someone looks like they are really happy to do this dare for me," Josh said with a chuckle.

Levi palmed his crotch. "Very happy indeed." He lowered his briefs to free his cock, revealing the strength of his desire.

Josh didn't say anything, his gaze locked on Levi's throbbing erection.

Levi went to pull his pants right down when a girl's voice called out. "Babe, are you home?"

Levi hauled his pants back up, sitting his arse back down.

Josh threw Levi a don't-say-anything glance. "Yeah, babe. I'm just in the lounge with Levi."

Little footsteps echoed from the kitchen until Jessica walked into the lounge, holding a bag of groceries. "Hi Levi."

Levi gave a friendly wave back, squirming his legs together to hide his arousal.

Jessica turned to Josh. "I just bought us some goodies for tonight."

"That's nice," Josh replied, his voice lacking any enthusiasm.

"I thought I could make you lunch and then we can snuggle up and eat chocolate together while we watch movies on the couch."

"Sounds perfect." Josh smiled up at her.

Jessica cast Levi an apologetic glance. "I'd offer to make lunch for you too, Levi, but I only bought enough for us. Sorry."

"Oh… that's okay." Levi wasn't hungry. Not for food anyway.

Jessica stroked Josh's shoulder with her nails. "I want to have you all to myself for as much as possible today and tonight. I can't believe you are being so naughty and going away for a holiday for so long without me."

"Yeah, sorry, babe," Josh said then said sorry with his eyes to Levi.

Jessica wasn't exactly being subtle, she wanted Levi gone. He sympathised, the girl probably knew how weak her grasp on Josh was so she wanted as much time with him as possible to try and win him over.

*It ain't happening.*

When Levi was sure his dick had died down enough, he stood up. "I guess I better start making tracks."

"You're still fine with feeding phoebe while I'm away?" Josh asked.

"Yeah, man."

"I told you I don't mind feeding Pheobe," Jessica said. "I love the adorable little girl."

"I would ask you, babe, but I know you're busy with work and Levi is free during the day to come check on her." Josh pouted at his *sort of* girlfriend. "But you're more than welcome to stroke me as much as you like when I get back."

"You know I will," Jessica purred.

"I'll leave you guys to it." Levi smiled and waved goodbye.

"Hey, Levi," Josh quickly said. "I'll leave that top of mine you wanted to borrow on my bed."

"The top?" Levi glanced back, clueless as to what top Josh was talking about.

"The one of mine you wanted to borrow." He gave a short, sharp sniff. "That one you've been wanting to try."

Levi's dick twitched, threatening to harden again. "Oh… yep. Thanks, man. That's really good of you."

"Yeah, I thought you might like to try it out before I get back. I don't think I've washed it though so it might be a bit whiffy."

Levi's pulse sped up, he was loving hearing Josh speak in code. "The whiffier the better."

Jessica sniggered. "Boys are gross."

Josh ignored her. "Send me an email and let me know what you think of it, okay?"

"I will. See ya." Levi raced out of the room before his dick pitched another tent.

Just as he walked outside, he heard Josh yell out. "Catch ya later, cum bucket."

# CHAPTER 9

Levi's balls ached and his dick throbbed, swimming in the pre-cum-soaked cloth of his underwear. Even though he had a bad case of blue balls, he still left Josh's place with a smile on his face. Very little had happened between them but enough had gone down that Levi knew he and Josh were moving towards a kinky zone where eventually he might have access to Josh's body in ways he'd dreamed of.

*I can't believe how keen he is for me to sniff his underwear.* That had been a shock. More shocking though was just how brave he'd been talking about it in front of Jessica. Admittedly she had no idea what they were actually on about but there was a rush from knowing Josh was willing to be a bit risky to get what he wanted—Levi's face inhaling his most private scent.

Levi wondered if it would be briefs or boxers waiting for him on Josh's bed when he went back to feed Phoebe tomorrow. He was hoping briefs but would be happy with either. Anything that had been wrapped around Josh's dick and balls was bound to be a sexy treat. The real hotness though would start when Josh got back from his holiday. Would he just want to see Levi sniff underwear? Or would he want to see Levi do a bit more than just that? The possibilities went from mild to wild but each one of them kept Levi's dick raging hard and oozing pre-cum.

The best part of all of this was knowing Dwight's nasty plan had backfired. Busting Levi tied naked to a bed with Cum Bucket written on his back hadn't scared Josh off at all. Instead it had opened his eyes to something he found appealing, sexy, and beautiful. Josh was so clueless he didn't even know what it was. But Levi did. Levi's best mate had a thing for control.

*Like father like son.*

Levi would make sure he fulfilled Josh's fantasies, and more. If he played his cards right then there was every chance he would have Josh's dick back in his mouth, Josh may even put it in his arse too. But what Levi wanted most of all, what he needed, was to have his own cock go balls-deep inside Josh's arse. Dwight would have a fucking fit to find out that his baby boy had bit the pillow and given up the goods. Levi wouldn't just fuck Josh once, he'd fuck him countless times, filling him with hot load after hot load and making sure he caught every moment on camera just so he could upload it to his blog where Dwight would see it. He would leave Josh's arse so wrecked that Dwight's own arsehole would twitch in sympathy.

He had driven halfway home when his mother's voice whispered in his ear, *Please, darling, can you just see if anyone knows anything.* The nagging guilt of not doing what his mother asked was enough to make him pull over and turn the car around, driving towards Brixton to fulfil his mother's wishes. If it was anyone else he would have just lied and said he'd done it but Levi didn't lie to his mother. He wasn't sure if she suspected anything about his wayward sexuality but if she bothered to ask then he would tell her the truth. At the end of the day they shared much darker secrets than where he chose to stick his cock.

*Like burying a body in an ancient Maori burial ground.* Levi smiled at the memory. Most thirteen-year-old kids would have been terrified of taking part in something a lot of New Zealanders would say was tapu. Not Levi. He'd found it liberating knowing he was finally free of the evillest man he'd ever known. He only regretted not spitting on his father's face before they started shovelling dirt over his bloodied corpse.

Levi smiled when he drove past Brixton intermediate. One of the few places in Brixton he remembered fondly. It was the place he met Josh for the first time. They'd bonded over a shared love of playing cricket at lunch time, Levi was pretty crap but the naturally sporty Josh excelled at it like he did at any sport he gave a go. After a while, lunchtime cricket led to hanging out after school and then weekend sleepovers until by the end of the term they were officially the best of friends and had been ever since. In hindsight, their friendship seemed so unlikely since Josh was not from Brixton.

Josh's mother, a social justice warrior ahead of her time, had taken Josh out of his perfectly good Fitzroy central school and sent him to Brixton intermediate so he could be exposed to people not from his own comfortable background.

Most kids from good families would have been a prime target for bullying at Brixton Intermediate but Josh fit in perfectly. He was that kind of guy. Likeable, non-judgemental and easy to get along with. Levi's two years at Brixton intermediate with Josh had been the best kind of distraction from the hurricane of abuse taking place in his own home during that time. Josh's friendship had been a lifeline, one he'd held onto for dear life. But that lifeline was taken away from him when it came time for them to attend high school. Josh's mother had decided against exposing her son to the even more dubious Brixton Senior School, and she enrolled him in a school closer to where they lived. Levi had been heartbroken at the time to lose his best friend at school but as fate had it, he would be reunited at the same school as Josh less than a year later when Levi's mother met Mark and the wealthy town planner asked them to move in with him. And thank fuck for that. Mark was an annoying schmuck—*with stinky balls*—but at least he was a good provider and had rescued them from poverty. The guy probably deserved a thank you for that but Levi would never give him one.

Levi glanced at his phone resting on the passenger's seat, contemplating pulling over and just texting Scott instead of visiting him. It would have been much easier to just text and ask the trashy dropkick if he'd heard from the equally trashy Shay. The thought of sitting in Scott's scummy flat for an hour and feigning interest in his povo life was painful to just think about but Levi knew the best way to find anything out about Shay was to ask Scott in person. It was highly unlikely Scott would give up any secrets he may know via text messaging.

Brixton boys had a weird loyalty amongst them. They may have badmouthed each other, stole from each other, or even fuck each other's girlfriends behind their backs but the one thing they didn't do was nark, so if Shay's *disappearance* had anything to do with another Brixton boy—which Levi strongly suspected it did in the form of a drug debt—then the only way Levi would find out is if he played the part of a Brixton boy himself, trying to ease Scott into a sense of security that Levi was just one of the gang and was more than happy to be ribbed about his cushy lifestyle.

Any time Levi visited his old childhood friends— and referring to any of them as friends was a bit of a fucking stretch—they made their jealousy over his easy lifestyle abundantly clear, taking cheap shots at his wealth under the guise of good-natured banter that wasn't actually all that good-natured. That is what made visiting anyone in Brixton more than a tad awkward. Well, it was awkward if Levi gave a shit what they thought of him—which he didn't. They could say what they like. At the end of the day most of them were penniless numbnuts living in rundown shitholes. And you didn't get much more penniless than Scott Miller—a hardcore stoner and perpetually unemployed fucktard.

Scott had been an awkward, funny-faced kid back in primary school who every one used to call "snotty scotty" on account of the sickly boy always having a runny nose. Now, as an adult, Scott had grown into his funny face and was almost cute. Emphasis on almost. He was still a tad on the runty side—not helped by his usual attire of sagging baggy pants and oversized hoodys—but a late growth spurt during puberty had at least gifted the jobless stoner an average height and a sexy voice that made him sound more masculine and confident than he perhaps really was.

Scott was friendly enough—friendlier than most of Levi's former childhood friends—but Levi hadn't seen him for over a year, not since he'd tested the power of money to explore his sexuality. Scott had been Levi's first experiment to see if he could get a straight guy to fool around for cash. It was imperative it be a straight guy, aside from the power kick Levi got from the idea of bending another person's sexuality to his will, he needed someone who he knew would keep their mouth shut. Scott Morris was the obvious choice for such a dubious venture. He was okay looking and his laidback stoner nature made Levi feel safe that if things didn't go to plan then Scott would at least not throw a punch.

Sure enough, no punches were thrown but that's not to say the usually chilled out Scott reacted well when first asked if he'd be keen to go gay for pay. Scott had grimaced and firmly said, "Fuck off, bro." His tune soon changed though when Levi opened his wallet and showed him the cash. The sight of money acted like a magical pacifier and was enough to convince Scott to give his body up for Levi's enjoyment.

It was a pitiful amount—fifty dollars—but Levi had purposely chosen to visit the jobless Scott the day before his doll payment which made the prospect of "easy money" much more appealing. Had Levi visited a day later when Scott had been paid, Levi doubted very much if his former childhood friend would have agreed to the dubious deal.

It had started nervously for both of them, standing in Scott's bedroom unsure of how to start things. After an awkwardly long silence with them both standing and staring at each other, Levi instructed Scott to take his clothes off and lay on the bed and to play with himself until his dick got hard. Levi had stood there, just enjoying the view of a naked male body, gently exploring Scott's smooth, slender body with soft strokes and tender touches.

When Levi had seen as much as he wanted, he'd upped the cash offer, giving Scott an extra fifty bucks if he agreed to suck Levi off. Again, Scott had struggled at first but after taking a minute to think it over he agreed and surrendered his mouth to Levi's cock, taking a series of brutal thrusts as Levi fucked the shit out of his face.

It had been a messy, amateurish blowjob but effective, culminating in Levi jizzing in Scott's mouth within five minutes. Scott had spat Levi's ball juice out over the carpet but Levi didn't care. It wasn't his bedroom floor getting messed up. He had simply put his dick away, buttoned his jeans, and turned and left without a word, leaving Scott naked on his knees with Levi's cum dribbling down his chin.

*Yep, gonna be an awkward visit.*

Scott probably wouldn't agree but the truth was he had gotten off lightly compared to the other guys who went on to be Candy Boy's future blog stars. Levi had been too nervous at the time to push Scott's limits too far but the other guys hadn't been so lucky, each one was made pose for numerous nude pictures while they performed degrading acts.

Inflicting humiliation on these guys was the ultimate thrill and went down well with Candy Boy's followers but there was another reason for making these Brixton boys endure such degrading kink. Silence. If it was just a picture or video of the guy having a wank then that would not necessarily guarantee he wouldn't tell others about Levi's interest in men, but if the guy was filmed on his hands and knees kissing Levi's bare feet, or pissing his own pants, then that made sure they knew it was in their best fucking interest to keep their mouths shut if they didn't want their mates seeing the images.

These videos of clueless, young, straight boys submitting to Levi's kinky orders had been a big hit with his followers, and he had fully-intended to make more of them. Unfortunately, he had grown cautious of this method after the last wanker (Twisted Candy) threatened to spill Candy Boy's secrets if Levi didn't agree to pay him more money. In hindsight it seemed crazy such blackmail hadn't happened sooner but Twisted Candy wasn't as stupid as the others, he had sniffed out Levi's intentions before anything was captured on tape which meant his silence couldn't be bought with the threat of humiliation. Well, that incident was enough to scare Levi out of trawling Brixton streets for other young hood rats looking to make "easy money."

When he parked in Scott's driveway, Levi took a deep breath, hoping he'd inhaled the patience he would need to sit through the dullness of what was to come. He climbed out of the car and made his way to the front porch to knock on the door but as soon as he raised his hand to knock, the door flew open and Levi found himself on the receiving end of a stoner's grin.

"Hey, bro. How are you?" Scott leaned a bare shoulder against the doorframe, his eyes bloodshot to buggery. He was half-naked, wearing only a pair of red silk boxers, his brown hair tousled and an overgrowth of stubble covering his jaw.

"I'm good man." Levi's gaze dipped to Scott's abs then back to his face, eyeing the scruff on Scott's jaw. "Are you growing a beard?"

Scott rubbed his stubbly face. "I've been trying to but I'm considering shaving it off 'cos I think it looks stupid."

"Nar, man. It looks good." Actually it did look sort of stupid but blunt honesty was not on the menu for this visit.

Scott stepped aside, waving one of his slender arms for Levi to come inside. "Come in, man."

As soon as Levi stepped inside the darkened flat, his nostrils were whacked with the stench of pot smoke. He cast a quick glance around the lounge. The curtains were pulled and the couch was covered with manky pillows and a ripped sleeping bag. In front of the couch was a wonky coffee table littered with an overflowing ashtray, a butchered cock bottle doubling as a bong, and three unopened packets of tailor-made cigarettes. Considering each packet cost about thirty bucks to buy, Levi figured they were most likely stolen.

A loud voice echoed from the hallway. "Who's at the door?"

"It's Levi," Scott yelled back.

Thumping footsteps made their way to the lounge and in walked Fergus Hurly, Scott's lanky best mate. Fergus was rocking a long-sleeved Metallica shirt, ripped black jeans and faded Dr. Martens boots. The clothes looked grubby and unclean like the man himself.

"Well, well, well," declared Fergus, his voice strained with resentment. "If it isn't Richie Rich."

"Yep." Levi forced out a smile. "The one and only."

"What brings you to our shitty part of the woods?" Fergus leered in Levi's direction.

"I was in the area and I thought I'd pop by and see how Scott was doing," Levi said, purposely excluding Fergus's name from the sentence.

Levi had hoped Scott would be home alone but he had half-expected Fergus to be here. He usually was. The 35-year-old Fergus had dated Scott's mother briefly about six years earlier and although the relationship was short-lived, he'd formed a close friendship with Scott in that time and they'd remained close ever since. The fourteen-year age gap between them might have made the pair seem unlikely friends but when you realised how thick Fergus was it made sense.

Fergus's weathered face was not blessed with beauty but he still managed to exude a certain kind of sex appeal some might find alluring. He had the look of a scowly brawler. Tall, shaved head, menacing dark eyes, and a slightly crooked nose from one too many fights. Adding to his don't-fuck-with-me image were badly drawn home-job tattoos on his neck and the back of his hands. He was always wearing jeans and long-sleeved shirts that made it impossible to tell what was underneath his clothes but whatever it was Levi assumed it would be unwashed.

Fergus swaggered over to the window, peering out a gap in the curtains towards the road. "You sure you wanna leave your fancy car parked out there? Can't have a rich boy like you having his toys get damaged."

"It's in the driveway so I'm sure it'll be fine," Levi replied.

"What is it? A Porsche Boxster?" Fergus asked, still peering out the window.

"Yep."

"Faaar," Fergus exclaimed. "Money bags much."

The sleek vehicle had previously belonged to Mark who—thanks to Levi's mother's persuasion—had gifted it to Levi as a present for his eighteenth birthday. It was a seriously nice car but Levi didn't like how it looked like something a man suffering a midlife crisis might drive.

Fergus made one final glance out the window. "I suppose it will be fine. We like the colour red out these ways."

"Good to know I'm colour-coded appropriately to please the local gangs," Levi said.

Scott laughed. Fergus didn't.

"Anybody want a drink?" Scott asked.

"Yep," Fergus answered immediately.

"Levi?" Scott stared at him.

"Uh, what do you have?"

"Homebrew bourbon."

"I think I'll pass, thanks." There was no way Levi was risking his liver on whatever rocket fuel Scott was serving.

"Don't be such a pussy," Fergus said.

"I have to drive back to town to pick my stepbrother up so I can't get hammered."

"Coffee?" Scott suggested as an alternative as he dozily scratched at his groin.

"Coffee will be great," Levi said, despite knowing the coffee would not be great. It was most likely the cheapest packet of coffee on sale aka coffee dust swept from the factory floor.

Levi took a seat on a wobbly looking stool while Fergus went and lounged on the couch which appeared to be doubling as his bed. They sat in stony silence for nearly two minutes until Levi finally asked, "Are you living here?"

"Nar. Just crashing at the moment." Fergus plucked a cigarette from one of the packet of smokes and lit it, taking a deep inhale. "I've been staying with my little sister but she's got a new boyfriend and they're fucking like rabbits and I'd rather not hear them."

Levi snicker-snorted.

"It ain't funny, man." Fergus grimaced. "The dude must have a ten-inch cock because he's got her screaming the fucking house down."

"You'd rather be here and listen to me have sex," Scott said as he walked into the room carrying a glass of bourbon for Fergus and a coffee for Levi.

"I'm staying here because this is the one place I know sex won't wake me up 'cos you never get any."

Scott laughed. "True that." He scurried off to the kitchen and returned with his own glass of toxic bourbon, settling on the couch beside Fergus.

Surveying both their faces, Levi decided this wasn't Scott or Fergus's first drink of the day. They weren't at slurring stages yet but they looked slightly flush. Scott more so than Fergus. Levi loathed being around drunk people when he was sober but he figured the booze might help loosen their lips when he got around to asking about Shay. But that would have to wait, he was about to endure an hour of boring chit-chat and not-so subtle digs about his wealth.

# CHAPTER 10

The hour passed like Levi imagined it would—dull and painfully drawn out. He pretty much just sat in silence listening to Scott and Fergus ramble on about bad mushy trips, breaking into cars and singing karaoke at the Brixton tavern. Boring topics in the best of times but when they were being discussed by two guys with less brain cells than they had fingers and toes then it was bordering on intolerable.

Naturally, there was a tonne of sly digs at Levi's wealth along the way with attacks made at his penchant for wearing designer labels, his "try-hard" car, and anything to do with his "bullshit pretentious" lifestyle. In previous visits, Scott and Fergus usually made equal amounts of digs at Levi's expense but this time Scott had laid off with the insults, preferring to just cough up laughter at whatever Fergus said. Scott must have been too worried about Levi bringing up their steamy interaction from over a year ago. The fuzzy-faced host needn't have worried, Levi had no interest in outing Scott because it would mean outing himself as well.

It was only when Fergus had started a conversation about his surprisingly active sex life that Levi began to take an interest in what was being said.

"Yep. But I think maybe my favourite part is making them suck my dick clean when I pull out," Fergus crowed proudly.

"Do you really do that?" Scott asked.

"Fuck yeah. That's part of a bitch's job."

Fergus's chauvinistic comment made Levi immediately think of Dwight and how the older man had given Levi the same degrading chore. A zip of arousal stung his balls and a zap of hurt whacked his heart. He suppressed his horniness and the hurt, forcing himself to focus instead on the anger he had towards his best friend's father.

"What if she tells you she won't suck it?" Scott asked.

"Trust me, bro. They never say no to my meat." Fergus waggled his eyebrows. "A cock as good as mine doesn't get rejected."

*We could have been perfect together,* Levi's inner voice said, still focusing on Dwight and his arse-breaking cock. Levi knew hot sex when he had it, and the way they had fucked had been hotter than any sex Levi had experienced in his life. Dwight Stephenson was a man who knew how to fuck. Levi would always be left wondering how good it might have been to not just fuck but to make love with such a brutally powerful alpha of a man. Levi hadn't made love since the last time he'd slept with Sophie, and for the first time in years, he wondered if maybe he missed being in love. But it was too late to get hung up on shit like that. Dwight Stephenson had betrayed him, humiliated him, nearly broken him, and there was a price to pay for that.

"What about you, Levi?" Fergus asked.

"Huh?" Levi frowned, unprepared to be lured from his Dwight daydream.

"Do you make the girl suck you clean when you pull out?"

"Uh… sometimes." Levi leaned back in his chair, hands over his stomach. "It depends on my mood."

"What's your favourite position? I'm guessing you rich boys only know missionary." Fergus laughed at his own unfunny joke.

"Doggy would be my favourite."

Fergus grinned, nodding. "Same as my bro Scotty here."

"Doggy all the way," Scott said enthusiastically, slipping a hand south to adjust his privates. "You can pound and spank 'em real good from behind."

"And you?" Levi asked Fergus.

"I know most guys think doggy is the best position but I prefer the chick riding me." Fergus's face locked in a serious expression. "I love playing with her tits while I hammer her pussy." His hands reached out in front of him, groping the air like he had a pair of invisible breasts to play with.

"Yeah, that's a good position too," Scott agreed.

Levi wasn't a mind reader but he was willing to bet Scott didn't have anywhere near the wealth of sexual experience Fergus did. Fergus spoke about sex with the confidence of a man who *knew* what he liked. Not like Scott who spoke with a hopeful wanting attached to his words.

"It also means I can look them in the eyes while they tell me how big my dick is." Fergus followed his arrogant words up with an orgasmic girly impression. "Ohhh, Fergus, Yeah. Fuck yeah, Fergus. Your dick is soooo big, baby. Mmm biggest I ever had."

Fergus and Scott fell into a fit of sniggering giggles.

"You must fuck a lot of liars," Scott teased when he'd finished laughing.

Fergus snorted. "Piss off. You know they don't have to lie."

"If you say so, bro." Scott gave his mate a playful nudge.

"They'd only be lying if I had a cock like your chubby little todger between my legs."

Levi's ears pricked up at hearing this. *Chubby little todger* was a pretty accurate description of Scott's dick. He wasn't *little* little but what he lacked in length he made up for in girth. When Levi had watched Scott stroke himself to full hardness, he remembered being impressed at how fat such a skinny bloke's cock could be.

"Have you seen each other's dicks?" Levi quirked an eyebrow.

"We have but don't get the wrong idea, Richie Rich," Fergus replied. "A couple years ago Scotty was dating this chick called Eve who had a thing for being serviced at both ends." He glanced at Scott. "She fucking loved being spit roasted. Aye, bro?"

Scott nodded.

*Finally. A decent story.*

"It was supposed to be a onetime thing to fulfil a fantasy for her but she kept asking Scotty to ask me to make an appearance in the bedroom," Fergus explained.

"That didn't bother you?" Levi stared at Scott.

"Nar, bro. I don't mind sharing my toys with this fella." Scott gave Fergus a quick one arm hug, spilling some of his own drink down his bare chest in the process.

"We're practically brothers so we're all good with sharing," Fergus said.

"Incestuous sharing." Levi nodded. "Classy." Neither boy picked up on his sarcasm. They were too pissed and stoned to notice. Considering their far gone state, Levi decided to be a little brave and dig for scandal. "Did Eve ever ask you two to fool around with each other?"

"Fuck no." Fergus scrunched his face up in disgust. "We ain't faggots."

"Nope. Definitely not faggots," Scott said, his bloodshot eyes drilling into Levi's gaze in a way that translated to *don't go there.*

"Well… I suppose there was one sort of faggy thing." Fergus snickered.

"What?" Scott frowned at his friend.

"You know…" Fergus licked his lips. "The tasty dish she asked you to eat."

Scott rolled his eyes. "That never actually happened."

"What didn't happen?" Levi asked.

Fergus leaned forward excitedly. "Sometimes after I'd dumped my load in her, Eve would ask me to leave the room so Scotty could clean up the mess. She said he was too shy to do it in front of me."

*That's fucking hot!* sounded in Levi's mind. He put his fingers to his mouth for a second just in case what he was thinking tried to leak out. He then laughed because he knew that was the appropriate response in this homophobic setting but that didn't stop his dick from twitching. The thought of Scott licking his best mate's spunk out of his girlfriend's cunt was some seriously sexy shit and for the first time since arriving, he allowed his gaze to graze over Scott's slim body that was so blatantly on show thanks to his lazy weekend attire of only wearing boxer shorts. Scott wasn't what anyone would consider a stud but his smooth torso and small nipples did have a lickable quality about them. As did his hair-dusted calves that showed off a line of toned definition each time he moved his legs.

"That never happened," Scott fired back.

"Don't lie. You know that's what she said, bro."

"Well, yeah, she may have *said* that but I never actually did it." Scott grimaced. "No fucking way would I ever lick up your cum dribbles."

"Aww, you might have liked how it tasted." Fergus patted the crotch of his jeans. "I'm often told how nice my swimmers taste."

Scott chuckled. "I severely doubt that, bro."

Levi suppressed a horny smile as Scott lifted his feet up onto the seat of the couch, spreading his legs wide open, and by doing so unwittingly gifting Levi a generous view up the leg holes of his boxer shorts. The erotic sight sent another erotic pulse up his shaft. Scott's legs were not too hairy above the knee and his inner thighs were a plane of smooth lightly-tanned skin that led up to the shadowy lumps of his ball bag. Scott then put his drink down and gripped his ankles, cementing his open-legged position in place. There was something intensely male about the way he sat with his legs spread so wide, an unashamed statement to the world that he had balls that needed to breathe.

Levi swallowed, reminding himself he was here for his mother not his dick. "Have either of you seen Shay Jacobs lately?"

Scott shook his head. "Nar, bro. I haven't seen him for about a month or two."

"He still lives in Brixton, yeah?" Levi asked.

"Not sure," Fergus said. "He's sort of missing."

"Missing?" Levi pretended to be surprised. "Has his drug debt finally got the better of him?"

"I honestly don't know," Fergus said glumly. "I hope not. Shay's a good cunt."

"You really think so?" When Levi saw the stern look on Fergus's face, he realised he'd said the wrong thing. Shay was well-known in Brixton and despite his illegal antics he was generally well-liked by those he didn't rip off or owe money to.

"Do you have a problem with him or something?" Fergus narrowed his dark eyes.

Levi shook his head. "Nar, man. No problem with Shay. I've barely seen him for years."

"Then you shouldn't make jokes about him being taken care of."

Levi shivered at *taken care of.* It very rarely happened but it wasn't unheard of for people to go missing who got themselves in trouble in Brixton. Ameesh had pretty much said the same thing earlier in the day.

The dark under belly of Fitzroy's worst suburb had more than its fair share of secrets, and while Levi had no way of knowing what all the secrets entailed, he had heard as a kid—from Shay himself—that some of these secrets lived in chopped up little pieces mixed in with farm fertiliser, and that other secrets had screamed their way down to the bottom of the ocean with a concrete block tied to their foot. Whatever the truth was, Levi was pretty sure their ends were ghastly.

Scott cleared his throat. "I don't know where Shay is at the moment either but I don't think he's been taken care of."

Levi glared at Scott, willing him to expand on what he'd just said.

"I sometimes score P off the same dealer so I know Shay had been in the shit with them but I got told he had paid them off in full about three months ago."

"How?" Fergus asked. "He's usually as skint as you and me." Fergus turned to Levi and snarkily added, "Just in case you don't know, Levi, but skint means poor, no money... something you rich cunts don't know anything about."

Levi rolled his eyes.

Scott dragged the topic back to Shay. "I thought you and your mum were really close to Shay?"

"We used to have a lot to do with him... when we lived in Brixton. He lived next door to us and he used to babysit me when Dad was out and Mum worked late shifts."

"I can't imagine Shay Jacobs as a babysitter. It's amazing you're still alive." Fergus laughed. "I bet he would have let you do what the fuck you want."

"Pretty much." Levi smiled, remembering his former role model. "He was rather liberal when in babysitter mode."

∞

As a kid Levi never thought of Shay as his babysitter, he viewed him as a friend or a cool big brother. He had been the one to teach Levi how to ride a bike, taught him how to shave—two years too early—and had been there for every major event in Levi's life. Yep, Shay Jacobs was family.

Shay, the blue-eyed rebel who oozed cool with his cigarette-smiles and give-no-shit attitude was the best babysitter you could hope for. He would let Levi stay up as late as he wanted, have shaving cream fights around the house, and always turned a blind eye to whatever naughty shit Levi did; like hurling waterbombs and eggs at passing traffic.

One of Levi's favourite memories of Shay stemmed from one of his most embarrassing—busting a thirteen-year-old Levi in the bathroom having a wank over the womenswear section of a Kmart catalogue. The awkward intrusion had sent Levi running red-faced to his bedroom and slamming the door, nearly in tears from being so embarrassed. He was horrified to be snapped doing something so dirty but what made it worse was he'd been caught dick-handed by the coolest person in the world.

After about five minutes of living in fear that Shay might think he was a pervert, a light knock sounded on the door and Shay casually entered the room and sat down on the bed beside Levi.

"I'm really sorry about before, LP. I should have knocked."

LP. *Little Prince.* A silly but sweet nickname Shay had called him for years.

"Yes you should have," Levi sulked, eyes aimed at the floor.

"I forget you're at that age. The little prince is growing up." Shay patted him on the back and said, "Don't be upset. Every guy in the world does it."

That's what the health nurse had said during puberty lessons but Levi wasn't sure how true that was so he'd asked Shay, "Even you?"

Shay had laughed and nodded. "Yep. Even me."

That had been a relief. If someone as awesome as Shay Jacobs tossed off then it must have been normal. "So you won't tell anyone what you saw me doing?"

"Of course not, egg. What you do with your stinky diddle is your business." He'd pretended to zip his mouth shut and throw away a key.

That had made Levi laugh and calm down. Shay was the one person in his life at the time who kept his promises.

"But we do need to get you some better material to work with." Shay screwed his face up like he'd just swallowed shit. "Wanking over a Kmart catalogue is just cruel."

The next time Shay visited he acted like nothing had ever happened, telling Levi when he left to go have a look under his bed. Levi had rushed to his bedroom wondering what Shay was talking about. He should have known. It was a box of porno mags, tonnes of them, all shiny and brand new. On top of the box was a note that read: **Happy reading Little Prince.**

Walking to school the next morning, tired and sore between the legs from staying up all night with his new reading material, Levi passed his local dairy and noticed a group of people congregated outside. Two men were boarding up the window while the shop owner stood outside explaining to an elderly man why the store wasn't open yet. "That's right, Abe. It's the second time this month we've been broken into. The filthy low lives took all the cigarettes again" He *tsked* in annoyance. "And they stole the bloody porno mags!"

It was crazy shit like that, robbing a store just to give Levi better wank material, that endeared the wayward older teen to a young and impressionable Levi. There was nothing Shay wouldn't do to make Levi's bleak life a little bit brighter or to keep him safe from harm.

He'd also been Levi's hero, the one person who'd stood up for him in the face of a deviant monster who ruled Levi and his mum's life with a drunken fist. But all those good feelings for Shay had been obliterated forever when they last spoke. Now whenever Levi thought of Shay Jacobs he just thought of a guy who had outgrown his cheeky rascal persona and had turned into an oversized thieving toddler with a bad drug habit, someone who, like Levi's father, was dead to him.

∞

The vibration of Fergus's cell phone on the coffee table snapped Levi out of his trip down memory lane. Fergus picked his phone up and began reading the text message, a big smile spreading across his lips.

"Just like I thought." Fergus said, a smirk forming on his lips. "She can't get enough of it."

Scott grinned. "Is that who I think it is?"

"Yeah, bro." Fergus handed Scott his phone so he could see. "I told you it'd happen again, didn't I?"

While Scott's eyes were busy reading the text message, Levi snuck another quick glimpse up the leg hole of Scott's boxer shorts, spotting one hairless nut dangling low. *Must have taken up manscaping since last year.* Levi was overcome with want, wishing Fergus would fuck off to his own home so he could proposition Scott and see what it felt having the drunk stoner's ballbag in his mouth.

It was a new feeling this, wanting to be the one on his knees sucking dick, sucking dick so hard that the guy lost his load and turned Levi's mouth into a lake of semen. Before submitting to the Stephenson men, Levi had always been the one flopping his cock out and expecting to be serviced but now he was just as turned on by the idea of being the one doing the servicing. He wasn't sure if he was resentful or grateful to Dwight for opening his eyes to a new kind of pleasure.

When Scott was finished reading the text, he handed Fergus back his phone. "Lucky bastard."

They both looked at Levi, expecting him to be curious as to what they were talking about. He wasn't. When he failed to say anything, Scott filled him in anyway.

"Do you remember Mrs Gower?"

"Nope."

"She was head of the maths department at Brixton High. Red head, big boobs," Scott said.

"She's been at the school forever," Fergus said. "Even when I was there."

Levi's mind drew a blank. He had only attended that school for a few months before his Mum met Mark and then enrolled him at the same high school as Josh. "I don't remember her."

"Well she's—" Scott began.

"I'm fucking her," Fergus interrupted. "Well, I'm about to fuck her. I was off my fucking face On Thursday night and sent her a message through Facebook telling her how much I used to wank thinking about her tits when I was at school."

Levi snorted. "Oh god..."

"I know right. Cringe as fuck. I just thought she'd block me aye, but nope. She sent me a message the next day inviting me for a cup of coffee," Fergus said. "One minute she was asking me how many sugars and the next I was asking her how many fingers." Fergus held up his phone. "The text I just got was her asking me if I would like to come over in an hour to finish what I started yesterday."

Levi studied Fergus's harsh face. He looked every one of his 35 years. "No offense, but if she taught you at school how old does that make her?"

Fergus sniggered. "Fifty-seven."

Levi couldn't help but smile. "Granny chaser much."

"Nar, bro. She ain't a granny... or if she is she's a fucking sexy one."

Scott nodded in agreeance. "Honestly, Levi, she's in good shape for a woman her age."

"She sure fucking is," Fergus crowed. "Got a very tidy minge on her too. And best of all, I don't have to wear a rubber because I can't get her pregnant."

Scott laughed. "Just as well. You don't want number eight."

"Do you have seven kids?" Levi was horrified.

Fergus nodded. "Seven that I know of. Could be more."

"Fucking hell," Levi exclaimed.

"Settle down, rich boy. If you fucked around as much as I did then you'd have a tribe too."

*No I wouldn't because I'm not a fucking idiot.*

Fergus tipped back the rest of his drink and belched loudly. "Is it all good Scotty if I use the shower before I go?"

"Knock yourself out, bro. My whare is your whare as they say."

"Cheers." Fergus stood up and lifted his shirt forward to take a sniff. "Yep. I'm pretty ripe."

Scott playfully whacked Fergus on the butt. "Go scrub ya box, manwhore."

"Will do," Fergus laughed. He let his gaze settle on Levi and said, "Good to see you, Buttwell."

Levi flinched at hearing his old surname. No one had called him that in years. He was so used to being a Candy that he sometimes forgot his old name even existed. "You too, Fergus. Have fun."

"I intend to." Fergus winked, groping his grotty crotch and leaving the room.

A few moments later, Levi heard the echo of gushing water coming from the bathroom down the hall. He eyed the barely-there blond hairs on Scott's legs, wishing so much he could lick his way all the way up to what was inside Scott's boxer shorts. But he pushed pesky sex thoughts out of his mind, telling himself it wasn't worth the risk of making a move with Fergus so close by.

Scott's stoned gaze fell on Levi, shooting him a dozy smile. "Have you been enjoying staring at my balls?"

"Uh, what? I-I haven't been looking."

"Yeah you have." Scott finally dropped his bare feet back to the floor, ending Levi's free perve. "I don't mind though."

"Sounds like maybe you wanted me to stare."

Scott shrugged. "Dunno. Maybe."

"Thanks for the view."

"Your welcome, bro, I remember you liked playing with my nuts last time you were here."

"I also quite liked fucking your face too."

Scott laughed, unfazed. "There's still a stain on the carpet from where I spat you out. I can show you it after Fergus has gone."

"Does Fergus know about what we did?"

"What do you think?" Scott stared at him like he was an idiot. "Fergus would have a fucking fit if he knew I'd sucked a guy's dick. He ain't a big fan of queers... no offense."

"None taken."

"So how much did you bring with you?" Scott asked, slipping a hand inside his boxers. "I'm happy for the same deal as last time."

Levi watched as Scott's hand began moving around in his boxers, making no secret of the fact he was playing with himself.

Scott pulled the front of his boxers down, exposing his semi-erect dick. "You can suck me off as well if you want." He squeezed his plump cock, making it harden some more. "I wouldn't charge extra for that."

"Sorry, but I didn't come here today to fool around."

"Bullshit." He put his dick away and gave Levi an ultra-serious stare. "You must have come here for something. You never visit me unless you want something."

"That's not true."

"Yeah it is. You usually only ever come see me when you want drugs."—he lowered his voice to a whisper—"or to fuck my face."

The paid sex thing had been a one off but Scott was right about Levi using him to get drugs. Whenever he was going to host a party, he'd come see Scott to hook him up but after using Scott for sex Levi had felt awkward about coming back so he'd found a new contact in the city, someone whose mouth he hadn't ejaculated in.

"That wasn't me being rude or nothing. I don't mind you using me," Scott said breezily, "Especially today."

Levi looked at the time on his phone. *3.55 p.m..* "I would be keen to play again but I've actually got to go pick my brother up soon so I don't really have the time."

"Are you sure? We could do something real quick. You got off pretty fast last time when I sucked you." Scott raked a fidgety hand through his messy hair. "And... and I'll swallow this time. I know I prefer it when chicks swallow me so I promise to do that. I really should have done that last time for you, sorry, but I hadn't expected you to shoot so quick but this time I'll be ready." His eyes pleaded with Levi. "I will swallow every drop, bro. Every fucking drop. Trust me."

The pathetic plea told Levi this was someone in desperate need of cash. "Why do you need money so bad?"

"I'm behind on my rent and the power bill is due in less than a week. I'm just so behind on everything."

"Fifty dollars won't solve all of that."

"One hundred," Scott flung back. "That's what you paid me last time."

"Oh... right. Well, one hundred won't solve all that either."

"It probably won't but it will give me enough to go out and get real fucked up to forget about my problems."

Levi laughed, pointing at the bong and glass of home brew. "Isn't that what you're already doing?"

"That shit is part of my daily diet." Scott chuckled. "I want to get something that's more of a treat. Don't you ever just have a shitty day or week and want to do something nice for yourself, even if it is a bit naughty?"

Until the promise of Josh being open to a new sort of friendship dynamic, the past week had been hellish, so Levi knew exactly what Scott meant. Usually when stuff wasn't going Levi's way he would just go out and blow money on some pointless crap or book a flight over to Sydney and party it up to make himself feel better, but money hadn't felt like it could fix the damage Dwight had done.

"Would you be keen to do more than last time?" Levi raised an eyebrow.

"You mean like getting fucked in the arse?"

"Yeah. And other stuff."

Scott let out a long, slow exhale. "I guess I could be into that for the right amount."

"What do you consider the right amount?"

"You tell me." Scott glared back.

"I asked first."

Scott nibbled his bottom lip, taking ages to answer the question, then winced when he finally coughed up a number. "300?" When Levi didn't respond, Scott quickly dropped the amount. "250?" And again. "Okay…200?" When Levi still didn't respond, Scott sounded pissy. "Fucking hell, man. Fine. You can fuck my arse and just pay what you did last time, but you gotta wear a rubber and promise me you'll go slow. I ain't had anything up there before."

There was something exhilarating about watching Scott gradually lower his worth, settling on a figure that was laughable. Levi knew that if he wanted to he could probably convince Scott to give his arse up for just fifty dollars. But as the shower echoed in the background, Levi decided he had a different purchase in mind.

"How about I offer you 500?"

Scott's eyes lit up like he'd just won lotto. "Fuck yeah. I'm down for that. Shit, I'll even let you blow your load in me for that much, bro." He laughed.

"But there's a catch."

"A catch?"

"It isn't me who will fuck you. It's Fergus."

Scott gaped. "What?"

"I will pay 500 dollars to watch you and Fergus have sex."

"Why the hell would you wanna watch that?"

That was a good question. They were such an unlikely pairing—one smooth and slender, the other busted and rough—but perhaps that was what made it so appealing. There would be a depraved thrill in watching Fergus skewer Scott's dainty arsehole with his dirty dick. Fergus didn't look like the kind of guy who knew how to wash his balls properly, or the kind of guy to show Scott mercy if Levi demanded he rub his sweaty sac in Scott's face. The experience would be nothing short of hugely unpleasant for Scott but hella erotic for Levi to sit and watch.

Rather than freak Scott out with the sadistic truth, Levi gave him a much simpler explanation. "Fergus talked himself up earlier like he was the king of fucking so I'd be keen to see him in action."

"He's the king of fucking chicks, not dudes."

"I'm sure you two could make it work."

Scott shook his head, frowning. "I don't think I could do that sort of thing with Fergus. He's my best mate... It'd just feel wrong."

"No one's putting a gun to your head, Scott, I'm just saying if you want 500 dollars then it's something you might want to consider."

"I know but don't you think it would be weird shagging my baby brother's father?"

Levi didn't even know Scott had a baby brother "Say what?"

"Fergus is Xavier's father."

"You're telling me that the man you tag teamed your ex-girlfriend with is also your brother's father?"

Scott nodded and wiped his nose roughly.

"Fucking hell, Scott. That's the kind of shit that could get you on the Jeremy Kyle show if it was still running."

"You're the one who wants to see me get fucked by him," Scott bit back.

"That was before I knew he was related to you— sort of related to you at least."

"Does that mean the offer is off the table?"

Levi was about to say forget about it all but he stopped himself, curious to see how low Scott was willing to go. "No. The offer is still there if you want it."

A storm of feelings blew across Scott's pensive face. "Let's say I was prepared to go through with it— which I'm not saying I am—but if I were keen, I don't see Fergus agreeing to it. He'd probably punch me if I even asked him."

"I think you of all people should know how open to suggestion a guy can be when there is money involved, and something tells me Fergus would be keen to get his hands on some easy money."

"There won't be nothing easy about that money."

"Will you even ask Fergus if he's keen?"

"I honestly don't know." The expression on Scott's face backed up his claim, he really did look unsure. "Is it okay if I take a few days to think it over?"

"Sure. No worries. There's no rush. My money isn't going anywhere."

"That must be nice," Scott said glumly. "Never worrying about bills and shit."

"It has its perks but you know what they say, money can't buy happiness."

"I've never had enough of it to find out."

The sadness of Scott's voice was enough to make Levi get to his feet. He didn't want to be brought down by other people's misery. He'd had enough of his own the past week. "Well, I better make a move. Danny will be a moany bitch if I'm late."

Scott promptly got to his feet as well, grabbing Levi's wrist as he walked past. "You sure you don't want a quickie before you go? Fergus takes ages in the shower so we probably have at least another ten minutes."

Levi studied the way Scott's hand wrapped around his wrist, gripping tightly. All he had to do was give the order, and Scott's boxers would be discarded in a heartbeat, his arse bent over the couch.

*But I can't… not yet.*

Levi had no problem with paying to watch Fergus and Scott fuck, but he was reluctant to take Scott right here right now. One day, yes. But not today. It wouldn't be fair to unleash the raging fury in his loins on the hapless Scott. The dopey stoner didn't deserve the fiery rage Levi intended to dish out when he finally fucked a man's arse for the first time.

Levi pulled his hand away from Scott's money-hungry grasp and reached into his back pocket. He dug out a fifty dollar note and handed it to Scott then walked towards the door to leave.

"Are you just letting me have this?"

Levi turned around and nodded. "Go do something nice for yourself… something a bit naughty."

# CHAPTER 11

If Levi's balls were blue before arriving at Scott's flat, they had turned purple by the time he'd left. It had taken all his strength not to cave to Scott's desperation and wreck his arsehole with a vicious fuck. Even though he was intending on saving his dick's first descent into an anus for Dwight's crusty old butt, Levi knew he still could have easily groped Scott's dick for a while before walking out the door, he probably could have even felt him up for free under the guise of paying at a later date. But even just a quick fumble of Scott's private parts felt wrong. Correction, it didn't just feel wrong, it was wrong, but Levi was used to doing wrong things all the time but in this instance he hadn't, and that surprised him.

Before he could congratulate himself on being a saint, his mind whispered to him, *You did do some wrong while you were there. Saying you'd pay money to watch Fergus fuck him.*

Yep. That was wrong. And it was a wrong Levi fully intended on going through with if Scott was ever silly enough to try and convince Fergus to go through with something that crazy. It would be great stupidity on their parts if they did go through with it, and because neither of them were the sharpest tools in the shed, Levi had a sneaky feeling it might just happen.

Sex was sex at the end of the day, and regardless if Scott and Fergus had to fake their way through a steamy encounter, the sex would still be toxic for their friendship.

Neither of them would have the brain power to navigate the emotional minefield that fucking each other would open up.

*Not like me and Josh.*

All sorts of relationships—friends, lovers, family—broke down through sex, even when actual sex wasn't even involved. Levi was going through this right now while trying to avoid his stepfather, and that was just from a pair of underwear... a pair of underwear that had smelled ridiculously sexy until Levi knew whose they were. Just the thought of it made him feel sick. If anything was going to make him move out of home then that might just be it.

By the time Levi was back in Fitzroy, he still had twenty minutes to waste before picking Danny up so he decided to take a detour into the city centre and browse the talent wandering the streets. He threw on his shades, and drove slowly, rubbernecking his way through the centre of town. The warm weather was a blessing, allowing him to enjoy the best of both worlds; girls in short skirts and the occasional shirtless guy. As nice as it was to see so much beauty on show, his favourite part of lapping town was the amount of people who looked back at him.

As he came to a stop at a set of traffic lights, a group of teenage girls who were sat outside a cafe began pointing at him and whispering until one of them broke rank and loudly declared, "He is so hot!"

One of the other girls scolded her shameless friend. "I think he heard you, Georgia. You're so embarrassing."

Levi gave them a wave, letting them know that, yes, he had heard them.

The girls burst into giggles as Georgia waved back to him.

Georgia was definitely the better looking of her friends, and apparently the most confident based on her volume and lowcut top.

*She looks familiar,* Levi thought to himself when he lifted his gaze from her breasts to her face. He couldn't work out where he knew her from but he had definitely seen that pretty face before. He got his answer when he saw a male version of Georgia—blonde, tanned and sporty-looking—walk out of the café and sit at the table with the girls.

*Brad!*

Georgia was Brad Kenny's little sister.

The Kenny family owned the largest dairy farm in the region, and Brad had thrown more than one party at his parents' country manor, parties where Levi had seen the young Georgia. This was before Brad had become a Benson Banger and banished from the in-crowd and exiled into social obscurity. Levi wondered if Georgia had any idea about her older brother's damaged reputation. Probably not, but in a year or two when she started attending Fitzroy Flyer functions, she would find out exactly what her brother was: a closet case bisexual who'd been busted letting Wade Benson nosh him off in the toilets at a party.

It was a shame Brad had fallen from grace, not because Levi particularly liked the guy, he didn't, but because Brad was husky, farm-boy masculine, and kind of cute. He wasn't what you'd call stunning but he was definitely one of the male Fitzroy Flyers Levi would have liked to have fun with naked. But not now. Benson Bangers were the lepers of Fitzroy's young elite and fucking one of them ran the risk of being tainted by them.

Levi turned to face the traffic lights, not wanting Brad to see him. It was one thing to chat with Brad at polytech—where they shared some of the same classes—but there was no way Levi was going to acknowledge his existence in the centre of town. Fuck that for a joke.

As soon as the light changed to green, Levi sped away to avoid any awkward interaction and made his way to Kaleb's house to pick Danny up. Kaleb only lived a couple suburbs out from the centre of town so before Levi knew it he was driving down a suburban street filled with rows of dilapidated state housing. The street was rough and rivalled Brixton with its poverty but the one thing it had going for it was just that… it wasn't Brixton.

Levi had picked Danny up from Kaleb's house a couple of times before but on account of all the orange-roofed weatherboard houses looking the bloody same he couldn't remember which house was Kaleb's. Thankfully Danny was already waiting outside on the footpath for him and flagged him down.

Dressed in black dress trousers, a white business shirt and his face adorned with thick rimmed glasses, Danny looked like a baby-faced accountant about to attend a business convention.

*Do you even know how geeky you look?*

The problem was Danny didn't seem to have a clue that the way he dressed made him look like a demented fucktard and that it was a large part of the reason he had been bullied right throughout high school. Danny thought he looked smart, going out of his way to try and dress like his father. But Danny failed to realise Mark only dressed that way when going to work, not the rest of the time. The only saving grace for Levi's stepbrother was at least his braces had come off six months ago and he now had a perfectly straight smile. Not that Danny would do much smiling at school, Levi imagined.

A huge grin appeared on Danny's face when he spotted Levi pulling over. He would always react like an overexcited puppy when Levi would pick him up. It was sort of sweet in a dorky way.

Danny raced over and jumped in the passenger's seat. "Hey, Levi."

"Hey, D-D-D-Danny."

Danny laughed. "I don't talk like that."

"I never said you did." Levi smirked. "I'm just so excited to have my day interrupted to be your uber driver that I can't help but st-st-st-stutter."

"Sorry. I thought Dad was coming to get me."

"It's okay. I didn't have anything else on." Levi did his best to sound genuinely unresentful. He put his foot down, revving the car's engine loud enough to make sure the whole street heard it then zoomed off.

"Where was Kaleb?" Levi asked.

"Inside."

"Why didn't he wait outside with you?"

"He did for a little while but he had to go back inside to help his mum with dinner."

"I bet."

Danny picked up the sarcasm in Levi's voice. "It's true. It's not like he's ashamed of being seen with me."

*If that's the case how come he doesn't hang out with you at school?* Levi didn't bother voicing this thought. He'd hit Danny up about it before but Danny would always come up with a reason to excuse Kaleb for his lousy behaviour, probably too worried that if he said one bad thing about the popular jock it might get back to him and he'd end up losing his one and only friend. But Kaleb Ladbrook wasn't Danny's friend. The guy was just a user who only hung out with Danny to benefit from Danny's generous allowance. Danny was always buying Kaleb shit like new clothes, video games and whatever else Kaleb desired. Danny was even paying for Kaleb to join him for his eighteenth birthday present; a seven day holiday in the South Island.

Naturally, Kaleb had jumped at the opportunity, probably thinking it would be a holiday spent in some luxury Queenstown resort doing cool shit like bungy jumping and white water rafting. That's what most young guys would want to do but *real* fun wasn't Danny's style. The birthday boy was actually planning a week-long trek through Fiordland National Park so he could go bird watching with his father. Danny had pleaded with Levi to join them but there was no fucking way Levi was walking all day with two of the most boring bastards in the world while getting bit to death by bloodthirsty mosquitos.

"What did you do today?" Danny asked, adjusting his glasses.

"I robbed a bank just after breakfast, caught piranhas for lunch, and this afternoon I fucked a Russian supermodel called Lana."

"Sounds like you had a busy day," Danny chuckled.

"You're telling me. My dick is almost bleeding from how tight Lana's pussy was."

Danny snorted. "Gross."

"I can't wait to tell your dad you think pussy is gross."

"No. It's your bleeding dick that is gross, knob-gobbler."

Levi laughed. "Knob-gobbler? Is that what you did today? Gobble Kaleb's knob."

"Ewww." Danny laughed. "No."

"So what did you do then?"

"I ate worms on toast for breakfast and after lunch I invented a secret potion that brings people back from the dead."

"Cool. And who are you going to bring back to life?"

"I was thinking maybe..." Danny sucked on his lower lip. "Bruce Lee."

"Why Bruce Lee?"

"So he could teach me how to kick ass. Hiii ya!" Danny sliced the air with a girly attempt of a karate chop.

"Shit. I better watch out or Karate kid might beat the shit out of me."

"I would never beat you up." Danny smiled at him.

It was only for a brief second but Levi noticed a sadness in Danny's smile, his usual dweeby spark wasn't sparkling.

"Is something wrong?" Levi asked.

Danny shook his head.

"Don't lie. I can tell something's wrong."

"How?"

"Because I can read your mind."

"Okay then, if you can read my mind tell me what I am thinking about right…"—Danny pinched his eyes shut—"now."

"You are thinking how you can't wait to get home and go to your bedroom so you can have a wank."

Danny's eyes flew open. "You're sex obsessed."

"But I'm not wrong." Levi indicated right, turning onto the motorway. "Now tell me. What's up?"

"Is it that obvious?"

"Not obvious but I can tell something's bothering you."

Danny sighed. "If I tell you, will you promise not to tell Dad?"

"Cross my heart and hope to die and all that bullshit."

"You really have to promise, Levi. I don't want him knowing or he will go stupid and contact the school."

"Okay, okay. I promise."

"When I was at Kaleb's house he showed me a website online called Verco's Virgins."

Levi knew all about Verco's Virgins. It was very much part of Verco High School tradition, a list compiling all the seniors who were suspected virgins. It had been around when Levi had attended the same school, and had probably been around in some other form before the invention of the internet.

"It's a website where people gossip about who they think are virgins at school and making fun of them for it and…" Danny struggled to finish the sentence.

"Your name was on the list?"

One look at Danny and you knew you were staring at a boy who'd not been near a vagina since his mum gave birth to him. He may have been the same height as Levi but thanks to his baby face and weedy physique he looked younger than his age and radiated innocence.

"Yeah…" Danny looked down at his feet. "Which is so stupid because as I told Kaleb I'm not even a virgin."

Levi nodded along, pretending to buy into Danny's lie.

"But what was most rude was that they started rating us…. the virgins… giving us marks out of a hundred as to how ugly we are."

*That part is new,* Levi thought. "What score did you get?"

"I got 93."

"Isn't that good? They might think you're a virgin but they think you're a hot virgin."

"You've got the rating around the wrong way. 100 is the ugly end of the scale."

"Ouch."

"I even got a worse score than Fabian Bedford and he was in a house fire as a child and is covered in scars."

"I wouldn't let it bring you down, buddy. They're just being cunts for the sake of it."

"You shouldn't say that word."

"And you shouldn't tell people what words they can and cannot say." Levi smirked. "If you let people say cunt a bit more it might help get you a better number."

"Har, har." Danny rolled his eyes. "Anyway, just promise you won't tell dad. I don't want him overreacting."

"I won't say a word." And Levi wouldn't. The last thing Danny needed was Mark calling up the school and demanding the students responsible be dragged into the principal's office which is exactly what Mark would do.

"Thank you." Danny folded his hands over his lap and went quiet.

They drove along in silence for a while until Levi felt the need to say something. "The kids are wrong you know. You're not ugly."

"I know," Danny said, not sounding like he believed it.

His stepbrother's glum response was heart breaking. More so because Danny had always seemed so comfortable in his own skin, blissfully unaware as to how geeky he really was. Levi felt like he was sitting in a car with a little kid who had just been told Father Christmas wasn't real.

"You're like me," Levi said, "an acquired taste."

"You're not an acquired taste. Everyone likes you."

"That's not true," Levi said, playing down how attractive he was for the first time in his life.

"Um, yeah it is." Danny looked him up and down. "Have you even seen yourself in a mirror?"

*About fifty times a day.*

"You're like the best-looking guy in town," Danny continued. "I don't know any guy who would be considered as sexy as you."

"Oooo. Somebody thinks I'm sexy." Levi teased his stepbrother by blowing him a kiss.

"I didn't mean it like that. I just meant that you're a very attractive guy—objectively speaking."

"You know, Danny, if you keep flattering me like this, I might just pop your cherry for you."

Danny snicker-snorted. "You're such a dork."

"Are you sure you're not keen to gobble the knob of the 'best looking guy in town?'"

"I'm not gay so I'm all good thanks."

Levi chuckled. "Yep. I know you're straight."

"How? Reading my mind again?"

"No. But I did read your internet search history on your laptop when you let me borrow it a few months ago."

Danny's face went bright red. "You better not of."

"Yep. Somebody sure digs his big-titted blondes getting spunked in the face."

Danny groaned into his hands. "This is so embarrassing."

"Chill out. Every dude looks up porn. You should see some of the nasty shit I look up online to get off to."

"Really?" Danny gazed at Levi. "What sort of nasty stuff?"

"Too nasty to tell you about."

"Yeah because it's probably gay porn." Danny smirked as if he'd just thrown the killer of comebacks.

"I've watched gay porn before," Levi said casually.

"What?" Danny shrieked. "You watch gay porn?"

"Haven't you? I get tired of watching the same shit."

Danny hesitated, looking out the window for a moment. "I watched it once. But just to see what the guys do. In someways it wasn't all that different to straight porn, I guess."

"Oh… I was meaning women licking each other out. That's what I meant by gay porn. Are you sure you're not a fag?"

Danny's face went blister red again. "I'm not gay. I swear! I did watch it but only because I accidentally clicked on the video when I typed in anal."

Levi laughed. "I'm joking, dipshit. I think most guys have looked up gay—as in two dudes fucking—porn."

"So before when *you* said you had watched gay porn you weren't just meaning lesbian porn?" Danny asked, probably assuming that if Levi said yes then it meant his own curiosity was completely normal. Which it was.

"Yes, Danny. I too have watched knob gobblers lift shirts and bash bums."

Danny laughed so hard he began to sound like a hyperactive walrus.

"Calm down, Karate kid. It wasn't that funny."

Danny gasped for breath, still laughing. "Yes it was."

Levi waited for the laughter to stop then ased, "Do you fancy Maccas for dinner?"

"What if your mum's made dinner for us?"

"Her and Mark are at a barbeque so you and I are fending for ourselves tonight."

"Okay then. A mac attack and two cheese burgers for me please."

"Are you sure you can eat all that?"

"Easily." Danny patted his stomach.

"I swear they need to study you to find a cure for weight loss. I've never known such a skinny terd who could eat so much."

Levi took the Green Meadows offramp, it was an exit too early for their suburb but where they lived lacked a McDonalds. The wealthy residents of Levi's suburb had campaigned against one opening in the area three years earlier on account of how the "garish bright logo would clash with the image of the area." *Pretentious pricks.* Levi

126

didn't usually mind pretentiousness, if anything he embraced it, but when it meant he had to drive fifteen minutes out of his way to get a fast food fix, he took issue.

Being 5.30 p.m. the drive thru was packed but Levi didn't mind. He hoped the tasty treat would help cheer Danny up. As they sat in line, waiting to reach the window to place their order, Danny chewed Levi's ear off about how excited he was about his eighteenth birthday coming up next Friday.

"It's going to be so awesome being eighteen. It means I'll be able to vote in the next election."

"That is the thing you are most excited about? What about being able to go to nightclubs?"

"Voting is better than going to nightclubs."

"If you say so," Levi mumbled.

"It's exciting knowing that my voice gets to be heard and help decide who runs the country." Danny nodded to himself. "It's an important part of being a democracy and we should all take part."

Levi sniggered.

"Why are you laughing?" Danny glared accusingly.

"Because voting doesn't matter to us."

"Of course it matters."

"We're rich, Danny. We don't have to worry about who's going to give us the best deal. We have so much money we don't need their deals."

"We're not rich," Danny said. "Dad's the one who is rich."

"Trust me, Danny. You and me are rich."

"But Dad's the one who earnt the money, not us."

Levi scoffed. "You do realise your mega rich grandparents gave him money to start him off, right?"

"Dad's still worked really hard and that's exactly what I intend to do."

"You need to worry less about shit like that and enjoy life."

"I do enjoy life."

"If you enjoy life so much how about instead of asking for a trip to some shitty national park so you can go hiking and explore the bird life"—Levi rolled his eyes—"you should ask your dad to pay for you to go party it up in Europe with birds that don't have feathers. That's what I did for my eighteenth, three weeks spent sunning and fucking on the Mediterranean."

It was Danny's turn to roll his eyes. "Not everyone wants pictures of themselves snorting cocaine off of some random girl's cleavage floating around Facebook."

Levi chuckled, remembering his epic eighteenth birthday party spent on a yacht off the coast of Spain. Those pictures had gotten him into a bunch of trouble with Mark when he got home but it was worth it.

"Sometimes it's good to get up to no good," Levi said. "It's about time you put your face in something that isn't a book."

"There's nothing wrong with me wanting to make my own money," Danny said, twisting the conversation back to money matters.

"You're even more loaded than me so stop stressing and have fun with it."

"How am I more loaded than you? We get the same allowance."

*We don't actually.* Levi always spent well above his generous monthly allowance but he always made sure his Mum paid the credit card bill before Mark saw it.

"You are richer than me because one day you will inherit Mark's and your grandparents estate."

"What about you?"

"Your dad won't leave me a dime."

"I wouldn't let that happen," Danny said earnestly. "But I still think we should both try and make our own way in the world without relying on our parents."

"Have I ever told you how much you sound like your father?"

"Loads of times." Danny smirked. "And I take it as a compliment every time. Dad's the best."

Had any other teenager uttered those words, Levi would have said they were taking the piss. Not Danny. He really did idolise his uptight conservative father.

"Maybe after I finish university you and me could start a business together."

"Why?" Levi asked, his eyes perusing the McDonalds menu board.

"So we can make our own money together."

"You're really hung up on that, aren't you?" Levi turned and glared snottily at his stepbrother.

"Sorry, sorry." Danny shot him puppy dog eyes. "Do you want me to change the topic?"

"Like you wouldn't believe."

"Okay." Danny smirked. "What are you getting me for my birthday?"

"If I tell you it will ruin the surprise."

"I don't mind."

"I was thinking of getting you a girlfriend."

"Really?" Danny's eyes widened. "Do you know a girl who likes me?"

"I do actually. But you'll have to make sure you save your breath after you've finished blowing out your candles otherwise she won't be any use."

Danny stared blankly, the joke flying over his head.

"I'm talking about a blow up doll, idiot."

Danny laughed, nudging Levi's arm. "That's mean."

"I actually don't know what I am getting you yet but I am sure it will be fucking awesome." Levi moved the car forward, and placed his order into the speaker box. "Can we grab a quarter pounder combo, two mac attack combos, and two cheeseburgers."

Danny waved four fingers in front of Levi's face.

"Sorry you better make that four cheese burgers. I have the world's biggest pig in the car with me." Levi drove forward, waiting to make his way to the window where he could pay for the meals.

"Did you wanna watch a movie together when we get home?" Danny asked.

"Um, what movie did you have in mind?"

"I don't care. You can choose."

"Somebody must be desperate to hang out if he's giving up movie choosing privileges."

"I like hanging out with you so I am happy to watch whatever you want." Danny's face soon lost its hope when Levi took too long to answer. "It's okay if you're busy. I keep forgetting it's a Saturday." Danny let out a humourless laugh. "You probably have a party to go to."

Levi always had a party to go to but he wasn't sure if he was in the mood to step out on the scene just yet. Maybe a movie night in with Danny would do him good. "Sure. We can watch a movie."

"Awesome!" Danny lifted his hand up to dish out a high five but Levi left it hanging.

"Sorry, Danny, but I don't do high fives."

"Aww, come on. Slap the hand, bitch."

"Who are you calling bitch, bitch."

"You bitch."

The car behind them suddenly tooted and Levi realised it was his turn to move up to the pay window. He eased the vehicle forward and stopped at the window and was greeted by a teenage boy with a name badge that said

Carl. The boy's hat wasn't on properly, slipping off to the side, showing off tight ringlets of blond curls underneath.

"That will be sixty-two-dollars-and-fifty-three-cents," Carl said in droll voice, handing over the eftpos machine.

Levi swiped his credit card and entered his four digit pin. He went to talk to Danny but Carl interrupted him. "Do you mind trying that again. It hasn't gone through."

"Okay." Levi swiped again, entered his pin and kept his eyes on the screen this time. Within seconds it flashed back with a word Levi hadn't seen in many years; *DECLINED.*

"What the fuck?" He tried another two times and each time it said the same thing. "There's something wrong with your machine, bro."

"I don't think so," Carl replied. "It's saying your card has no money."

"Bullshit. Have you seen what kind of car we are driving? Do we look like the kind of people who have cards that decline?"

Carl shrugged, completely disinterested in arguing. "Look, sir, if you don't have the funds to pay then I am going to have to ask you to pull out of the drive thru so the other *paying* customers can come through."

"Don't get cheeky, curly sue. We could buy shitty store if we wanted to with our fucking pocket money. And you'd be the first one I'd fire."

"Oh god," Danny groaned, slinking down.

"Look, sir, do you have another card with money on it, if you don't then I suggest you drive on because I am not here to put up with your abuse."

"You know what, Carl, how about you suck my—"

"Just use my card," Danny blurted, jabbing his credit card into Levi's arm.

"Are you sure you want to buy from here after the rude service we have received?"

Danny's face was red. "Please don't make a scene. Just pay for dinner. I'm starving."

"Fine. What's your pin number?"

"Cheque. 0123"

Levi entered it in and the card accepted.

"Thank you, sir. Please drive on to the next window."

"Thank you, Carl," Levi said loudly and sarcastically.

"That was so shameful," Danny whined. "I can't believe you just did that."

"He needs to pull his head in. It's obvious their machine is broken and yet he's fucking telling me I'm some broke arse bitch with no money. If only the little prick knew how much money was on my card."

"Just because we're rich doesn't mean we have to be rude."

"Chill out."

"They are probably gonna spit in our food now."

Levi rolled his eyes. "No one is gonna spit on our food."

"They might even snot into our burgers… or spoof in our drinks."

"Lucky us." Levi licked his lips. "Extra vitamins."

Danny grimaced. "You really are feral."

"And you really are a sweet little man with a hardon for me."

"What are you on about?"

"Your pin number. That's my birthday. December the 3rd."

"Don't flatter yourself. It's just an easy number to remember because it is counting upwards. 0,1,2,3."

"But you're not denying it's my birthday?"

"Yes, Levi, it's your birthday."

"Aww. That really is so cute." Levi ruffled Danny's hair.

Danny pulled his head away, giggling like a girl. "Shut up."

When they got to the last window to collect their food Levi was surprised to see Carl appear again. "We meet again," Levi groaned. "I thought you were working the other window?"

Carl handed over their drinks and bags of food. "I was but I switched so I could give you this." The teen's hand dipped into his pants pocket and reappeared with what looked like a small business card. "It has my number on my back... just in case you want me to suck your..."

Danny gasped, holding in a laugh.

Levi smirked. "Thank you, Carl. I take it all back. You are a customer service super star."

"So does that mean you'd be keen for a date then?" Carl grinned.

"I would but..." Levi rubbed Danny's thigh. "I've already got a boyfriend."

Danny's mouth farted out giggles.

Carl smiled. "Damn."

"Have a good night, Carl," Levi gave the kid a wave goodbye and drove off.

Just before they left earshot of the window, Levi heard the curly-haired blond boy call out, "You too, *daddy*."

# CHAPTER 12

"Why would he call me daddy?" Levi asked Danny for at least the tenth time as they sat and ate their McDonalds together on one of the oversized comfy couches in the family lounge. "Do you think this Carl knows me?"

"I told you, he was probably just being funny." Danny chewed down on one of his cheese burgers. "Why are you so stressy about it?"

*Because I am looking for a blond guy who fucked me, one that I called daddy while mistakenly assuming it was my best friend's father.*

"It just pisses me off."

"Why are you pissed off? You weren't the one who had his thigh molested." Danny grinned at him.

"You should be thanking me, that's probably the closest a hand that isn't your own has ever been near your dick."

"No it's not."

Rather than debate Danny about the boy's imaginary sex life, Levi asked him again. "So you don't think he knew me?"

Danny exhaled loudly as if he were sick of the topic. "If it's annoying you so badly why don't you just text him. He did give you his number."

*Why didn't I think of that?* "That's a good idea."

"You know what would also be a good idea?" Danny pointed towards Levi's phone on the table. "Check your credit card balance and make sure it was the machines mistake and not yours."

"I know the machine was wrong because there is no way I have spent fifteen grand this month."

"Why do you even have such a high credit limit? That's ridiculous."

"The credit card company keep offering to increase the limit so I just say yes. It's not like I ever spend that much in a month. I always keep it under five grand."

"Five grand!" Danny squawked.

"That's actually really good considering how expensive it is to be me." Levi knew he sounded like a twat but it was expensive being him.

"What the heck do you spend that much money on each month?"

"Clothes, shoes, concerts, trips away, restaurants, nights out and—" He stopped himself just before he said drugs—"And I like to be generous with my friends."

"Wow." Danny shook his head. "I didn't realise you spent so much."

"It's fine. It gets paid every month and Mum and Mark get the reward points."

"That's so generous of you to give them the reward points you earn from using *their* money."

It bugged Levi to hear Danny trying to lecture him on money management but he appreciated his stepbrother referring to the money in the house as belonging to both Danny's father and Levi's mother. That was kind, even if it was untrue. Every cent that came into this house was Mark's, Levi's mother—like Levi—just helped spend it.

Levi saw Danny's mouth move like he was about to continue his lecture about money. "Before you start yapping, I am checking the balance now." Levi's fingers were like lightening on his phone's touch screen, logging into his credit card account in seconds.

*What. The. Fuck!*

He was so stunned he repeated his thoughts aloud. "What. The. Fuck?" A sickly chill raced up his spine. This was bad. This was really fucking bad.

"What is it?"

"It says…" Lei stopped himself from saying what the balance was but he was too slow to move his phone away before his stepbrother saw the balance on the screen.

Danny dropped his burger. "Oh my God, Levi. What have you been buying?"

"It must be wrong. It has to be. I've been good this month."

Danny sniggered. "I think you and Dad might have different versions of what 'good' means."

"Fuck up, Danny. This isn't funny."

"No it's not," Danny said seriously. "Dad is going to have a hernia when he finds out."

"He won't find out if you keep your mouth shut."

"You can't not tell him. He's the one who has to pay it."

"Mum pays it for me."

"She can't just pay out that much and not tell Dad about it."

"She spends way more on herself and never has to ask for his permission."

"Because she is his wife. You're not." Danny shook his head, striking a parental frown of disapproval just like his father often did. "It's best to be honest in these situations rather than—"

"Just shut up for a moment," Levi snapped. "I'm trying to see where the money's gone." He clicked on the list of transactions. There it was. First page. A purchase of nearly ten grand. Levi gulped. "Fuck. Fuckity, fuck, fuck. Somebody's been using my credit card."

"Can you see what they've used it for?" Danny asked.

"They've used it to buy a... luxury holiday package." A wicked wooziness came over him. He took a deep breath, trying to gain control of his muzzy brain.

*You dirty, fucking, lowlife, raping, old-as-the-hills, waste-of-fucking-space, white trash, sweaty dick motherfucker!*

"I have to go." Levi put his McDonalds down and stood up, racing into the kitchen where he'd left his car keys.

"Where are you going?" Danny yelled.

"Out!" Levi called back, grabbing his keys from the kitchen table, then sprinting back to see Danny in the lounge. "I'm just letting you know that I might be out rather late."

"How late?"

"I don't know. But remember, don't tell Mark anything. I will sort this, okay?"

Danny nodded. "Okay."

"Promise me, Danny. You can't tell your father."

"I promise, bro."

Levi would have laughed at how lame Danny had said the word *bro* but there was no time for laughter. There was only time for revenge. Dwight Stephenson was about to finally discover hell hath no fury like a Candy Boy scorned.

∞

Levi gripped the steering wheel with white-knuckled fists, his heart pumping with vengeful purpose as he sped his way to Dwight's house. Once he was out of the city limits, he really floored it, reaching dizzying speeds that would kill him instantly if he failed to take one of the numerous bends on the dark country roads. But he didn't care. He was too damn furious to give a shit if he hurt himself, he was only focused on hurting Dwight.

"You fucking thief!" Levi screamed as he drove along. "I am going to chop every one of your fingers off and feed them to the possums." He wasn't sure if possums would eat human flesh but some creature in the surrounding forest would eat Dwight's fingers and shit them out.

Levi had no idea how Dwight had managed to use his credit card to book a luxury holiday package through an online travel agent. Who else could it be? It was too much of a coincidence that Josh had told him earlier in the day about the three week vacation his father was taking him on. Levi knew at the time there was no legal way Dwight could afford such an extravagant purchase but he had never once thought it was his credit card that had paid for it.

*But how did he get access?* Levi brainstormed, trying to work out how Dwight could use his credit card details online. The credit card lived in his wallet and Dwight would never have been able… *Oh fuck.*

Levi's heart squeezed as he remembered being tied to his bed for Dwight to fuck him. Josh's father had arrived earlier than expected that day, interrupting Levi in the middle of shopping online with his credit card to buy new clothes.

"I forgot to put anything away. I fucking forgot."

Not only had Dwight used Levi's credit card, he'd probably used Levi's laptop to make the purchase which added salt to the wound. Levi was now angry with himself for being so stupid to let a known crook inside the house, allowing the man to tie him to the bed and then wander freely wherever he liked. Levi knew he should have expected someone like Dwight to do something like this. Josh's father might have loathed anyone from Brixton but he was just as much of a criminal as someone like Shay Jacobs.

More than once on the drive he considered pulling over and calling the police and dobbing Dwight in for theft, but each time he slowed down to do it, Levi pictured Josh's excited face. He didn't want to rob Josh of the holiday of a lifetime, especially not when he was so close to flying out.

But there was another reason, a much more selfish one, why Levi wouldn't and couldn't call the police. If he dobbed Dwight in then Dwight would probably retaliate by showing everyone what was on the hidden camera, Levi's shameless moans for *daddy* to go harder and deeper. If that video got out he would be the laughing stock of the whole town, not to mention he would lose his place at the top of the social scene.

Levi was so distracted with his thoughts that he nearly drove straight past Dwight's house. He slammed on the breaks to stop in time, skidding onto the side of the road. For a brief moment he worried if such a commotion would attract unwanted attention but luckily Dwight didn't have any neighbours living nearby. The nearest house to Dwight's rundown shitheap was at least a kilometre farther up the lonely coastal road.

Levi stepped out of his car, the summer sun slowly dipping over the horizon as he marched up the driveway towards Dwight's house. Each step he took closer to the front door, Levi could feel a dark monster cutting up his soul, desperate to claw itself free from its cage and unleash agony on a diabolical scale. Levi knew this monster very well. He'd embraced it at thirteen when he stood over his father's bleeding body, gripping a knife in his hand as he wished hell upon the cruellest man he'd ever known. Levi had let the monster out of its cage that night just to survive but he had promptly locked it up again, hiding it away like the bloodstained shirt in his closet, scared of what it made him capable of. *Anything.* But it was time to let the monster out again and let it do whatever it needed to.

It was only now that he was standing, pounding on the door, demanding Dwight come outside that Levi remembered Josh saying Dwight had already left to go to Auckland to fly out. "Fuck!" Levi screamed, genuinely gutted to miss his chance to deal justice to a man who deserved it.

Levi went around to the back of the house, making his way to an old door that came off the laundry room. He stripped his t-shirt off, wrapped it around his fist and punched through one of the glass panels on the door. Glass crashed down, shattering inside the house. He fished his hand through the hole he'd made and unlocked the door to let himself in.

Levi felt like a passenger inside his own body, merely a spectator to what was going on as he walked through the laundry, into the kitchen and then the lounge. He stood for a moment, gazing at the scruffy old couch where he had lost his anal virginity to a man he never knew he found so insanely attractive until that night. Not only had that evening opened Levi's eyes to Dwight's rugged sex appeal for the first time, it also opened his mind to the erotic world of submission. He wasn't sure if he hated Dwight more for making him bend over and be his bitch or for making him enjoy it.

As humiliating as it had been submitting to a man he despised, a part of Levi had gotten off on being forced to take every inch of dick the older man had, he'd even enjoyed kissing Dwight's feet and being made say thank you for the supposed honour.

Levi strolled down the hall and went into Dwight's bedroom and switched on the light, casting a soft yellow glow over Dwight's messy bed. A black duvet was laying on the floor and the white sheets were tangled at the bottom of the mattress, strings of rope still attached to the bed posts at the end of the bed. Levi wandered over to Dwight's wardrobe to see if he could find any secrets like a bloodstained shirt.

There were secrets in there, just not murderous ones.

"Fucking hell," Levi gasped. "You kinky motherfucker."

His gaze was captivated by the two top shelves filled with dildos and butt-plugs, in every size, shape and colour. They stood erect like an army of toy soldiers waiting eagerly to be plucked off the shelf, coated with lube and firmly pressed into action. Lower down was yet another two shelves filled with kinky apparatus: Fleshlights, nipple clamps, gags, cock rings, whips and chains. Most scandalous of all was a metal cage built into the back of the closet. The cage was small and only high enough for a person to crouch in with barely enough room to turn around. Inside the cage was a dog bowl filled with water and a half-eaten muesli bar, indicating it had recently been used. Levi wondered if Blondie had been in here. Or maybe even Aroha. He wasn't sure if he felt relieved or jealous not to have been locked away and abused with Dwight's toys.

Once Levi was finished with the Christian Grey museum, he began scouring the house looking for the hidden camera. If he could find that then maybe he would be able to see who Blondie was and never be at Dwight's blackmail mercy again.

Levi searched everywhere, cupboards, drawers, under furniture; he left nothing unturned in his pursuit of that camera but his search yielded nothing. When he was done trying to find it, he sat down in one of the armchairs in the lounge and chucked his t-shirt back on. His gaze fell on the couch again, his hearth thumping with a toxic rage while his dick debated whether to harden over the memory of what had happened in that spot.

Levi knew there was a good chance he would visit here again with Josh, having to pretend everything was fine, but how could he do that when he would have to sit in this lounge and look at that couch without feeling in some way inferior to the man who owned it. It would never be just a piece of furniture to Levi, it would be a sacred place where his masculinity had been slaughtered and his heart held captive. The whole fucking house was like that.

*It has to go. It ALL has to go.*

He wandered into the kitchen and hunted down a roll of paper towels in the pantry. He took them with him back to the lounge, fetched his lighter out of his pocket and began to set bits of paper alight, dropping them over the couch until eventually the ratty old thing was a stage for dancing yellow flames. When the flames grew so high that they set the nearby curtains on fire, Levi hurried outside and stood on the lawn to watch Dwight's house slowly catch ablaze. It was a beautiful sight, deep reds and oranges peeping through the windows, billows of smoke climbing to the dusking sky above.

A quiver of grief skittered along Levi's jaw and burned the backs of his eyes. Tears soon fell freely, wetting his cheeks as he mourned for a man he stupidly thought could save him from himself. Had he loved Dwight? No, he hadn't. But Dwight had received love from him in the form of trust and a heart willing to open up to the possibilities of a future where an openness about who Levi really was could have been comforted.

Levi knew it was crazy to feel so strongly for someone after just a couple dirty, brutal fucks but Dwight's touch had elicited something deep and personal within him, coaxing his heart out of a slumber it had been in since ex-girlfriend Sophie had dumped him nearly four years ago.

In some ways the love Levi had felt for Sophie had stayed with him after they broke up. He had carried it around with him, sharing it when he felt the need to be warm towards another person. It was never anything extravagant, just small signs of affection like a smile, a pat on the back, or a compliment. The small things. It was Sophie who was responsible for these rare moments of affection, not himself. But after everything Dwight had done to him, the man had taken the last of the love Levi had saved from Sophie. There was no more left to give.

His heart was empty now.

# CHAPTER 13

The whole way home Levi was spookily calm for someone who'd just committed arson on a serious level. Instead of being worried or upset, he was actually happy about what he'd done. It felt good to finally get one over on Dwight Stephenson and pay the man back for the disgusting way he'd treated him. Levi smiled each time he imagined the distraught look on Dwight's face when he came home from his holiday and discovered he had nowhere to live. The trashy fuck would probably have to go live in a caravan park, surrounded by crazy spinsters with too many cats.

On the way home Levi made a detour back to the Green Meadows McDonalds, going through the drive thru to order a frozen yoghurt just to see if Carl was still working. When he got to the first window to pay for his desert, he was disappointed to not see Carl there. He paid for his frozen yoghurt with coins from his glovebox then drove on to the next window to collect his purchase.

"Back so soon," said Carl when he recognised Levi.

Levi smiled, pleased to see his Blondie suspect was still working. "Yep. Back again."

"Where's your boyfriend?"

"My *boyfriend* is at home."

"I hope he doesn't mind you coming back here to flirt with me," Carl said cheekily.

"What he doesn't know won't hurt him," Levi replied, grabbing his frozen yoghurt from Carl. "Hey, um, I just wanted to ask… do you have any tattoos?"

"No." The boy frowned. "Why?"

"You wouldn't mind if I asked to see your lower back just to make sure?"

"Random." Carl laughed.

"Can I see?"

"What? Right here?"

Levi nodded, shooting him a flirtatious grin.

"Okay then, sexy." The boy untucked his work shirt and turned around, flashing Levi a smooth tailbone free of any sinister markings.

*Bugger.* Levi couldn't decide if he was relieved or annoyed to not be staring at the distinctive DS tattoo. On one hand it was annoying to still not know the identity of the person who'd treated his arse like a sperm bank but on the other hand it was a relief to not be hurling out rape accusations in the middle of a McDonald's drive thru.

"Thanks for that," Levi said.

"That's okay, sexy." Carl tucked his shirt back in and turned to face him again. "Maybe we can play some more show and tell later, if you know what I mean."

Levi humoured him with a laugh. "One more question. Why did you call me daddy earlier?"

"Huh?"

"When I was here earlier, you called me daddy as we drove off."

"No I…" Carl's eyes slowly lit up. "I didn't call you daddy. I called you Paddy."

"Paddy?"

Carl pointed at Levi's chest. "Your t-shirt. It has a four leaf clover. Irish. Paddy."

"Oh." Levi felt like an idiot.

"But I am more than fine with calling you daddy if you prefer."

"I definitely don't prefer."

"Should I be expecting a call from you later?" Carl asked.

"I don't think my *boyfriend* would appreciate that."

"I won't tell him if you won't."

"I'm sure you won't," Levi said, driving on with no intention to ever lay eyes on Carl again.

∞

Levi was surprised to see his stepfathers Mercedes in the garage when he arrived home. Mark may have whinged earlier about how he didn't want to go to the barbeque but the man was an extrovert at heart and loved social outings, often being one of the last to leave any dinner party he and Levi's mother attended. Either the hosts had wanted an early night or the dinner party must have been painfully boring that they chose to bail after eating.

Levi casually strolled inside, preparing to use Peach as his excuse for having just gone out. Peach would cover for him if anybody asked. She wasn't above lying for him and had done so many times before.

"Hey, man." Levi smiled at his stepbrother still sitting in the lounge.

Danny paused the movie he was watching. "Where'd you go?"

"I went and saw Peach."

"Really? You looked like you were about to murder someone when you left."

"Uh, no. I just... I forgot that I hadn't dropped off somethings she'd leant me."

"What did she lend you?"

"Mind your own bees wax," Levi said. "Where's your dad?"

"Right here," growled Mark's voice.

Levi spun around and saw his stepfather walking in from the hallway. He was in shorts and t-shirt, perspiration dripping down his face.

"You can't get enough of that treadmill can you, Forest Gump," Levi teased.

"I'm not in the mood for your jokes, Levi." Mark marched over and stood so close that Levi could smell the sweat on him. "You and me need to have a very serious talk."

Mark didn't have to say what it was about, it was obvious he knew about the credit card.

"You little fucking nark." Levi flashed Danny a filthy look.

Danny promptly shot up from the couch and scarpered out of the room.

"Fucking, Judas!" Levi yelled out.

"Leave Danny out of this," Mark snapped. "You're the one in trouble here."

Levi's mother suddenly appeared, rushing in from the kitchen to see what was going on. "What's all the fuss about?"

"Danny informed me earlier that Levi here has wracked up a fifteen thousand dollar credit card bill."

"Oh…" Levi's mother clutched her chest. "Fifteen thousand?" She stared at Levi seeking confirmation.

"It's not as bad as you think," Levi replied.

"How could it not be as bad as I think?" Mark said angrily. "You have either gone and spent fifteen thousand dollars or you haven't. Now which is it?" Mark's unforgiving gaze demanded an answer.

Levi flirted with the idea of telling the truth about how Dwight had stolen the money. He felt confident that

147

the camera had been burned within the house but he couldn't be sure. "I shouted Josh and his father a holiday to Bali for Josh's birthday."

"Why on earth would you do something so stupidly outlandish?" Mark's expression twisted in outrage.

"It was his twenty-first birthday. I figured he deserved something nice."

"Me and your mother had already done something nice by covering the cost of Josh's birthday party. An overseas holiday that expensive is just ludicrous, especially when it isn't your money to be generous with."

"It's my credit card," Levi said.

"Yes, which *my* money pays for each month," Mark fired back, spit flying out of his mouth.

"Say it don't spray it." Levi wiped his face and took a step backwards.

"I strongly suggest you start watching your tone." Mark stepped forward and jabbed a finger in Levi's chest.

An outpouring of adrenaline hit Levi's system, boosting his heart rate and blood pressure. "If you want to hit me, Mark, just hit me. Don't be such a fucking bitch about it."

The tension was rife. Levi knew that if either one of them moved an inch right now then they would lock bodies in a fit of swinging fists and nasty kicks. But Levi was ready. He wasn't scared of his stepfather.

Levi's mother ran and stood between them, pushing at their chests to try and separate them. "Both of you just calm down. I won't have any violence in this house."

Mark's glower darted to Levi's mother. His eyes softened for a moment then returned to Levi, reigniting with fire. "No one is getting violent, Jenny." Anger chopped his breaths. "We are just having a wee chat."

"If that's the case how about we all go to the kitchen and discuss this like adults," Levi's mother suggested. "I am sure we can come to some sort of solution."

"I love you, darling, but you need to butt out on this one." Mark's cold blue eyes drilled into Levi's mean hazel gaze. "Me and Levi need to talk alone. Man to man."

"Why? So you can slap me in the face with a glove and challenge me to a dual?" Levi laughed under his breath but there was no humour in it. "Fucking faggot."

Mark's nostrils flared and his hands balled into fists.

"Stop it you two," Levi's mother said. "I am not going anywhere until both of you are sat down at opposite ends of the room."

Mark was the first to step away, taking a seat on the couch.

"Now you too," she said to Levi.

"Fine," Levi mumbled, going and sitting down on the chair farthest from the couch.

Levi's mother stayed standing there, refusing to budge.

"It's fine, Jenny. No one is going to be fighting here tonight," Mark said, feigning calmness.

"Yeah, cause you're a fucking pussy," Levi snorted.

"Levi," his mother snapped. "Stop it." She looked at Mark. "Is it okay for me to go now?"

"It's fine, Jenny," Mark said through gritted teeth.

She didn't look sure how true that was but she left the room anyway.

Tension still clotted the room but the risk of a physical solution to their argument had passed. They were about to battle how they usually did; with nasty words.

"I want to apologise for how heated everything just got," Mark said, not sounding like he meant it. "But you have really annoyed me Levi. I mean *really* annoyed me."

"There's nothing new about that."

"Oh, believe me when I tell you this is new, I have never been so angry and disappointed with you before."

Levi went to snap back but he stopped himself, knowing it would be better to apologise and just get on with life. Mark was the man with the money after all. "Look, I'm sorry for not asking you first before I paid for the trip but I promise it won't happen again. I just wasn't thinking."

"That's your problem, Levi. You never think. You spend copious amounts of money each month with no appreciation into what has gone into earning that money."

"I said I'm sorry."

"I'm afraid that sorry isn't good enough this time." Mark stood up and slowly approached Levi's chair, stopping far enough away as to not encroach on Levi's personal space. "I want you to give me your credit card."

"Why?"

"I think you know why?" Mark held his hand out expectantly, waiting for Levi to cough up the card.

"I'm not giving you my credit card.".

"Yes. You are."

Levi sat stoically, refusing to budge.

"Either you give me your credit card or I will take it off of you." Mark stepped closer, this time standing well within Levi's personal space, towering over him as he oozed a masculinity Levi didn't know the man was capable of.

Levi weighed up his options. Do as he was asked, or stand up and fight. He wasn't scared of Mark but something about his stepfather's stance made him submit to his demands. "Fine," Levi said. He rolled his eyes and pulled his wallet out of his pocket and handed over his credit card.

"Thank you," Mark said, walking back to the couch to sit down. "You won't be getting this back until I feel you have earnt it."

"And how do I earn it back?"

"By doing exactly what I want," Mark said, sounding creepier than he perhaps intended.

"If you're expecting me to suck your dick then I will expect a much higher limit on the card when you give it back."

Mark's face wrinkled with revulsion. "Don't be so disgusting."

"Chill out. It's a joke."

"I don't care what it was, just try and keep your mind out of the gutter for just one second." Mark shook his head, sighing. "What I want you to do is to grow up and be a man and stop leeching off me and your mother for support which means get out there and get a job and start paying for your own stuff."

"I can't get a job because I am studying."

"Don't give me that nonsense. We both know your course is a waste of time and you barely attend any classes. The only reason you got through the first year is because I made a large donation to the polytech for a new library and the tutor was forced to pass you."

"Really?" This was news to Levi.

"I am sick and tired of paying for you to live the life of some spoilt little brat."

"You never keep tabs on Danny's allowance."

"I don't keep tabs on Danny's allowance because I don't have to. He never spends as much money as you do. Never!"

"Because he's a fucking loser who never does anything."

"Or maybe he is sensible and rather than waste his money he actually saves it." Mark paused, scratching his thigh. "While you've been out shopping like some Beverly Hills housewife, Danny has been saving his money. You should probably consider doing the same."

"I can't now because you're cancelling my allowance." Levi shrugged. "But whatever. I know I can't compete with golden boy nark-a-lot."

"Don't even try and insinuate that I pick favourites. I have always done my best to treat you and your brother equally."

"That narking little prick isn't my brother."

"So you keep saying, Levi." Mark exhaled loudly. "If anyone doesn't treat others equally, it is you. You're the one hung up on how me and Danny are not really your family yet you expect us all to treat you like royalty. Well, guess what? You're not royalty. You are just a conniving little snot who time and time again proves to me why I cannot trust you."

"Gee, Mark. Don't stop there. Tell me how you really feel."

"You are a lazy, self-centred, vain, nasty little punk who I am sick of supporting."

Levi laughed. "Fuck, man. I was being sarcastic. You didn't have to actually expand on the reasons you hate me."

"I don't hate you. I love you. I know you don't see me as your father but I do see you as my son and it hurts me to see someone with so much potential just waste it."

"If you love me so much then you'll let me have the credit card back."

Mark shook his head. "Not happening. I expect you to go out and get a job and start paying your own way."

"You're actually serious about me getting a job?"

"Of course. How else will you be able to start paying me and your mother board for staying living here."

"What the fuck? You expect me to pay board?"

"You have two weeks to find a job and start paying us some board. And I mean reasonable board, not a pittance."

"And what if I don't?"

"Then I suggest you sign up for the dole and go see if you can live with your father's side of the family instead."

"But they can't stand me."

"That seems to be a recurring theme with you."

"Screw you too."

Mark ignored the insult. "And to make sure you really learn your lesson, I will be selling the Porsche to pay for the money you owe me."

"Fuck off." Levi's eyes bugged. "You're not selling my car."

"I think you will find the car is mine, Levi. It's in my name. And don't tell me to F off in my own home."

"But you gave me that car for my eighteenth birthday. You said I could treat it as my own."

"I know… and now I am taking it back."

"Don't be such a fucking spaz, Mark. That car is worth way more than the money I've spent this month."

"I am sure it is. Maybe I will use whatever is left over to pay for a holiday of my own."

"You are such a fucking dick."

"A dick who is forcing you to finally take some responsibility for his actions. This is for your own good, Levi."

"And this is for yours," Levi hissed, pulling the fingers.

"Don't get your knickers in a twist. I'm not that nasty that I would expect you to go without any form of transport."

"What are you going to get me? An imaginary bicycle?"

Mark chuckled to himself and stood up. "Two weeks, Levi. Two weeks." He pivoted and left the room.

Levi just sat there, stunned. Mark had never laid the law down like this before. He usually just whinged and moaned about Levi's lifestyle but never did anything about it. Sure, this month had seen a hefty amount spent on the credit card but it wasn't like Mark couldn't afford to pay the bill.

*Fucking prick.*

Levi remained seated for a moment, wondering what the hell he could do. There really was only one solution. *Mum.* Levi got up and went into the kitchen where he found his mother having a herbal tea at the table.

"Is everything okay?" she asked.

Levi slumped down in a chair at the table, resting his head in his hands. "Mark's confiscated my credit card and expects me to start paying board."

"Oh dear." She smiled softly. "That's not good."

"Can you talk to him and just tell him to stop being a dick."

"I don't think that will work, darling."

"Why? It always works. Whenever he's being a dick, you tell him to pull his head in and he does what he's told." Levi pretended to crack a whip. "You have him trained."

She laughed. "I don't think I have him as well-trained as you like to think."

"Can you talk to him?"

His mother didn't speak for a moment, a look of quiet contemplation over her face. "I will see what I can do but it might also be a good idea to take his advice and get a job."

"Are you serious?"

She nodded. "It might be a good time for you to be planning ahead."

"Planning ahead?"

"For a time when maybe we won't have Mark and his money to fall back on."

"Why does that sound so ominous?" Levi sat up straight. "Are you and Mark having problems?"

"No, dear. Nothing like that." She may have been smiling but a small twitch of her jaw gave away she was lying. "What I am trying to say is no one can see the future and what it holds for all of us. There may come a day when you might need to stand on your own two feet and it is better you start planning for it now while you have some say in the matter. We both know how cruel surprises can be."

Levi gulped, nodding. He wanted to ask what she really meant but he was too scared to know the answer.

# CHAPTER 14

*Hi everyone,*

*The past four days have been a fucking nightmare in my house. My stepfather has confiscated my credit card and replaced my car with a Nissan March. If you don't know what that is just picture a shit heap on wheels and you'll get the idea.*

*Now I am sure most of you don't give a shit about my situation at home and are probably just thinking 'show us your dick, Candy Boy' but it has a lot to do with why I am writing this post. Usually I don't care who pays to view my private content but because of my current money situation I am for the first time needing you fine folk to really support me and sign up for my next Candy Boy masterpiece. If you have ever considered paying for my exclusive content then now would be the best time to do it. Not only will you get access to the hot posts I already have there but you will get to be the first to read the juiciest and most taboo story I have ever written. Full disclosure, the fuck I intend to be writing about hasn't happened yet but it will be soon.*

*And what is this supposedly hot story I am talking of? It is a story about me seducing a piece of Forbidden Candy. And why is it forbidden? Because the piece of Candy just happens to be my little brother. And do you want to know what is best of all? He is a virgin!*

*Now before you all go getting preachy and reporting me for incest I better tell you that we're not related by blood. He is my stepbrother. Still, it feels weird knowing I plan on sticking my dick in someone I have had to refer to as my little brother for the past 8 years.*

*But he has it coming and deserves to go to school with a sore arse. Trust me on that one.*

*I wouldn't say he's that hot but if you like them young then Lil D (that will be his code name) will be right up your alley. He's a skinny boy and is the same height as me. I think he is the same shoe size as me too but I will find out for you. You know I give every detail I can. He has black hair, wears nerdy glasses and looks young for his age. He turns eighteen this week! If all goes to plan then my present to him will be popping his cherry.*

*Now I know my last couple hook ups haven't exactly gone to plan but this time I won't fail. This time I will finally stick my dick inside another guy's arse. I am taking the plunge if Lil D likes it or not. And why am I so determined? Because he has pissed me off and I need the cash. Simple as that really. I have no shame admitting that.*

*As you all know, I tell the truth. That's what I do. This isn't some fake arse bullshit like 99% of the blogs on here. So you can all rest assured that when I tell you this boy is my stepbrother he really is my stepbrother. Not only will I describe every single detail I will go out of my way to get more pictures than ever before. I want you all to get value for money and I promise you that this fuck will be a lot of value for money.*

*Take it easy you wonderful crazy horny fuckers.*

*Candy Boy.*

Levi read over his short blog post one last time before uploading it. He hoped it would entice his followers to pay for his next private story. It wasn't the most well-written or steamy plea for money on the site but it had some of the essential ingredients to make it work. *Stepbrother. Teenage boy. Virgin.* Hotly sought-after aspects when it came to anything erotic on the Crashing Hearts site. Levi wasn't attracted to Danny in the slightest but the kid was a guaranteed money maker which meant Levi would gladly rise to the occasion.

With Mark taking away his credit card, Candy Boy was Levi's only source of income. The alternative was to go out and get a real job but fuck that. Levi wasn't about to go be a peasant in the fields just to please his stepfather. He'd rather fuck the man's son and profit off of that.

Levi's blog had always proved popular but he'd never treated it like a business despite its potential to make money. He needed Candy Boy to go from earning several hundred a month to several thousand. Such a big jump was unlikely straight away but he knew with the right kind of story that he could bring in enough to at least pay Mark some board and earn a little play money for himself. And Forbidden Candy was the right kind of story.

The thought of Danny having sex with anyone was just downright weird, the boy had a purity about him like a Disney character. But Levi wasn't letting that stop him from using his kid brother to fatten his wallet. Any pangs of guilt Levi may have had were silenced when he reminded himself that Danny was the reason he was without his allowance. If the four-eyed geek had just kept his mouth shut then none of this would be happening. Danny only had himself to blame for his sphincter's impending doom.

Danny being straight was the least of Levi's worries, the boy's sexuality was an inconvenience more than anything else, it wasn't something often talked about but plenty of hetero guys had secret stories about that one time they got a bit gay with a mate. The biggest challenge would be trying to create the right kind of situation that would allow for them to do some *exploring* as Levi liked to call it. Danny didn't drink alcohol which didn't help, the kid didn't do much of anything that would help Levi lure him into a false sense of security where their clothes could come off. But he would think of something…

Levi was about to shut his laptop down when a message came through on the blog site from *Demon Dave*. "About fucking time you replied." Levi clicked into the message, wondering if Dwight had decided to confess to being Demon Dave. He hadn't.

**I'm sorry Candy Boy but I believe you have me confused with someone else. Who is this Dwight?**

Levi quickly flicked a message back.

**Stop playing games Dwight. I know it's you ya thieving cunt.**

Within seconds, Demon Dave responded.

**I don't take kindly to being called a liar and a thief Candy Boy.**

Levi rolled his eyes and sent back another message.

**If you aren't Dwight then how come you know I live in Fitzroy? I suggest you quit the bullshit and just tell me who Blondie is.**

Levi sat and waited for a response but one never came. "That's right, Dwight. I know it's you." Levi resisted the urge to send another message, informing Dwight his house had burned down and that Levi had spent the past few days sniffing his son's underwear. Most people would have been more horrified about losing their most valuable asset but Dwight Stephenson would have probably have been just as horrified to know his only son was dabbling in kink with Levi.

Josh hadn't been lying when he said he'd leave a pair of underwear on his bed for Levi to sniff. There had even been a cheeky little note left on top of the white Calvin Klein trunks that said: **I did an extra set of sit ups just for you xx**

The kisses were jokey of course but that hadn't stopped Levi hoping they were real. He'd stripped all his clothes off laid down on Josh's bed, wadding the briefs up and cramming them against his nose and open mouth, inhaling Josh's scent. He sniffed the strong smell of sweat buried in Josh's underwear while he jerked off and fantasised about what else Josh might be willing to explore when he returned from his holiday. It had been an excellent wank that culminated with cum splattering all over Levi's stomach and Josh's sheets which he then wiped up with one of his socks. It had been totally worth walking around with a squishy foot for the rest of the day.

If there had been one downer about it all, and it was only a slight one, it was that the lingering smell of Josh's ball sweat failed to take him to the same musky nirvana he'd been to when Dwight had tied him to the bed and blindfolded him with a pair of Mark's underwear. The thought was fucking gross that the smell he associated with such erotic bliss actually belonged to his stepfather but Levi knew it had nothing to do with Mark and everything to do with Dwight. Josh's father was such a sexually-charged monster that anything he touched turned to sexy, even a pathetic middle-aged man's gruts.

Levi's inbox glowed red with a new message. Dwight had finally decided to message back. Levi clicked into the message, surprised by what he read.

**You and I have never met Candy Boy but I must say I would love to see you in the flesh and do naughty things to you. *Twisted* things like this…**

Levi noticed there was a link at the bottom of the email, curiosity got the better of him and he clicked on the link and was taken to a video of a dark room. There was nothing naughty about it… just a dark room with a rattling sound in the background. But as the person recording the video rounded a corner and entered a new room, one lit with dim red lights, Levi's cock took notice of what he saw.

There was a naked man suspended from some sort of scaffolding contraption. He dangled there in the position one might imagine superman flying. Feet tied at one end, his arms stretched out in front of him with his hands firmly tied like his feet were. He was wriggling and writhing uncontrollably, trying to break free from his restraints while he mumbled and moaned. When the camera got closer, Levi saw why the man was robbed of the ability to formulate proper words and why he was making so much damn noise. Over his face was a gag-like mask while over his cock was a plastic tube that beat up and down at a furious rate, milking all the cum out of his body. The machine was going so fast that Levi worried if it was gonna rip the man's cock right off. The camera did a close up of the tube, showing the copious amount of jizz gathering in the tube.

The man didn't need to say words for Levi to understand what he was enduring. It was the height of pain and pleasure combined. Heaven and hell. He was experiencing both the joy and punishment of sin at once, one second his body would flex in gasping pleasure and the very next he would grunt and jolt in pain.

"Fuck me," Levi muttered, squeezing his dick through his pants.

The camera moved down to the man's feet and zoomed in closer, showing all the detail of his lithe body. His feet were slender and long with skinny toes that couldn't stop curling, his hair-dusted calves and thighs rippled with lines of definition each time he tensed, the dusting of hair stopped halfway up his thighs, giving way to smoother skin. The camera leapt forward, trailing the underside of the man's body. His cock was too covered by the pump to show the size of his milked manhood but the tube was beginning to leak fluid. Some of it didn't even look like cum, it was so clear and watery it could have even been urine. The man's stomach had a wide snail trail that thinned out above his bellybutton before spanning out again over his pecs. Each time he clenched his stomach, the valleys between his abs became more pronounced. This was a guy with a seriously good body, and Levi absorbed every detail he could, his dick reacting so positively that he had to pull it out of his pants and start wanking. He didn't usually get into BDSM vids like this but something about how helpless this poor man was triggered a primal instinct within Levi. Whoever it was recording this was undoubtedly a predator and the guy suspended was the prey. The whole video had a vibe of doom about it, like something worse was about to happen but Levi cast those concerns aside, too turned on by the dark and raw nature of the video. Levi didn't care if Demon Dave was Dwight or not, whoever they were would be getting a big thank you message from Levi for sharing such an insanely hot video—after he'd finished jerking off, of course.

He was only moments away from ejaculating all over his computer desk when the camera suddenly veered up and zoomed in on the dangling man's masked face. Levi let go of his dick in fright when he saw the bluest eyes he had ever seen on another person staring back at him.

Eyes that belonged to Shay Jacobs AKA *Twisted Candy*.

# CHAPTER 15

Levi got such a shock that he slammed his laptop shut. Had he never seen those eyes then he would never have known the dangling man was his childhood idol. It sent shivers down his spine, prickling the hairs on his arms. *How the fuck did Shay end up in a video like that?* Levi had no idea but he was willing to bet it was because of Shay that Demon Dave knew he lived in Fitzroy.

If he wasn't so terrified about the prospect that the video was actually some sort of snuff film then he would have logged back in and kept watching it. He'd always fantasised about seeing Shay naked, and now he had—mostly.

In many ways, paying Brixton boys for sex had all been in a bid to build up the confidence to get the one Brixton boy he had always wanted. Shay Jacobs. It wasn't until Levi began sexually experimenting with other guys that he even realised that a large part of the reason he'd always looked up to Shay was because he'd had a crush on him as a kid. A crush he'd kept for all these years. It seemed silly in hindsight not to recognise it years sooner considering for how long Shay had appeared in Levi's fantasies.

The perverted thoughts started when Levi was thirteen, after Shay had saved Levi from his monster of a father. They'd started sort of innocently, things like imagining what it would be like to kiss and cuddle Shay, as

Levi got older though the thoughts became steamier, more perverse and by the time he was sixteen, and even though he was dating Sophie, Levi would often wank at night and think about what it would feel like to fuck Shay Jacobs and taste his dick. Many a sock was corrupted with Shay's name on it.

So when Levi finally made the decision to explore his sexuality past a supposed "one-off" drunken blowjob, he always knew that Shay was the ultimate catch. Shay was the one who'd been his protector as a kid and for some fucked-up reason Levi found the idea of protection incredibly attractive. And to an impressionable 13-year-old at the time the crush began, you couldn't find anyone more protective than the neighbourhood rebel with a heart of gold.

He should have known better. The dream image he had of his childhood saviour was not one based on reality. Shay wasn't some Brixton version of Robin Hood, he was just some drug-fucked snake who stole from the rich and the poor. He didn't care where he got money from, just as long as he could feed his meth habit.

Levi winced as he remembered how badly his eventual move on Shay had gone, a story that had so much promise but went down as his worst Candy Boy story up to that point. *Twisted Candy.* It didn't just go wrong, it backfired like flames out of a Nasa space shuttle, burning Levi to a crisp. Rather than secure the prize of Shay's mouth on his dick, Levi was forced by Shay to stop trawling Brixton streets and paying hard-up straight boys for sex. Instead, he wound up paying Shay for his silence. It wasn't heaps of money at first, but it slowly climbed, getting more and more as each week passed. Then, when it got to the point that Levi seriously worried if he could continue to afford buying Shay's silence, Shay just disappeared. There were no more texts, no more phone calls. Just utter silence.

*Until now.*

Levi knew that the video was of a darker nature. He could feel it in his bones. And while he knew the *right* thing to do was to contact the police and show them the video, Levi wasn't prepared to do that. He probably owed Shay a lifesaving moment or two but Shay had lost those privileges. Not just for the blackmail, but for the unforgivable things Shay had said to him *that day*. The day Shay became Twisted Candy. They were heartbreaking words that could never be taken back and try as Levi might, he could never unhear them. Assuming Shay was still alive then it was up to Shay to rescue himself. Levi wasn't in the business of helping others, especially others who had broken his heart.

He opened his laptop back up and went to Demon Dave's message. Rather than watch Shay's erotic torture again, he deleted the video from his messages. He had no use for it. Shay may very well still have been alive but it didn't change the fact he was dead to Levi.

*Let him fucking rot.*

∞

Mouth-watering smells of dinner wafted in the air as Levi entered the kitchen and saw his mother stirring a wooden spoon in a pot on the stove. For a split-second he considered mentioning the video but decided better of it. He'd already told her Scott's story about how he was sure Shay was still alive. That had calmed Levi's mother down. The video would only worry her again. What was the point in that?

"What are you cooking?" Levi asked.

His mother spun around. "Blue cheese sauce." She pointed at the oven. "It's to go with the chicken breasts I have on."

"Smells delicious," Levi said.

When Levi's mother began dating Mark, he had a personal chef who would come and prepare meals for him each night but Levi's mum was a whiz in the kitchen and had taken over cooking dinner soon after they moved in. Mark had been surprised by her talent but years of learning to be creative with little money for food had taught Levi's mum a trick or two.

"Delicious enough for you to stay and have dinner with us?" she asked.

"I can't sorry. I have plans."

"What plans are more important than dinner?"

"I have to go feed Josh's cat, then I am going to go visit Peach."

He hadn't seen Peach in nearly two weeks and the pink-haired gossip journalist was getting impatient with him, she had called him up earlier in the day and demanded he visit her apartment that evening for an overdue catch up.

"Tell Peach I say hi," Levi's mother said.

"Will do."

"Are you sure you don't want to stay and have just a small bite to eat with us before you go?"

"I would but I don't want to be at the same table with fuckface."

His mother sighed. "I know you are still angry with Mark but he has apologised to you." She smiled. "Perhaps it is time you at least start talking to him again."

It was true. Mark had apologised for the spat they'd had, approaching Levi the very next morning to say sorry for anything he may have said that was hurtful and to explain why he still expected Levi to get a job. Levi had been making his way downstairs at the time when Mark spotted him in the upstairs hallway and walked out of his bedroom in just his underwear to say sorry. The sight of his stepfather's body had left Levi's gut squirming, the half-naked attire was made worse by the fact Mark had been wearing the same green briefs Dwight had tied to Levi's face. The whole time Mark spoke to him, scratching his hairy chest while he prattled on about the "wonderful" benefits of getting a job, Levi swore he could smell Mark's pungent balls. Obviously he couldn't actually smell them but just the glimpse of Mark's package was enough to make him relive the musky scent that was forever etched into his memory. He ended up interrupting Mark's spiel with a dismissive grunt and raced down the stairs, desperate to get away.

"He wasn't sorry enough to give me back my credit card," Levi said sulkily.

"Maybe if you start being nice to him then he will."

Levi snorted. "I doubt it. He has it in his head that getting a job will 'make a man out of me.'"

Levi's mother smiled. "I know to you and I that kind of talk might seem a bit—"

"Bullshit?" Levi offered.

"I was going to say old school, but yes, it can be that also." She chuckled. "But Mark does mean well. I wouldn't have married him if I didn't think he had your best interests at heart."

*Yet you stayed with my father who didn't.*

"Have you tried talking to him for me?" Levi gave her an expectant gaze.

"Not really."

"Why?"

"Because things are a little complicated at the moment."

"I thought you said you two weren't having any problems?"

"We aren't." She blinked rapidly. "We're just… it's complicated."

"How is it complicated?" Levi knew he was pushing harder than he should but his mother was the only person who could talk Mark into reinstating his credit card."

She sighed, obviously annoyed but still smiling. "Unless you want to hear about our sex life then you might want to just leave it at complicated."

Levi grimaced, raising his hands. "You're right. Sorry. I shouldn't have pried."

"That's one way to keep you quiet," she quipped.

"I will never push you for information again."

"Good." She smiled. "Now are you sure you don't want to stay for dinner."

Levi shook his head. "No thanks. I'm definitely not hungry after hearing that."

He was about to leave the kitchen when his mother called out. "Levi, one more thing."

He pivoted, facing his Mum's direction. "Yeah?"

"Have you bought Danny a present yet?"

"No."

"His birthday is tomorrow, you haven't got long."

"In case you forgot, I don't exactly have much cash on me at the moment."

She placed the wooden spoon down and walked over to her purse sitting on the island bench. She pulled out one of her credit cards. "Use this. But don't go crazy with it, like buying him a trip to Bali."

Levi laughed. "It would be cheaper with Danny because I'd only be buying a one-way ticket."

She swatted his arm playfully. "Don't be silly."

Levi eyed his mother's credit card, an idea coming to him. "Is it okay if I hold onto this until Friday?"

"Why Friday?"

"I was thinking I could pick him up after school and shout him a Danny day out. You know, take him to the art gallery, maybe see a movie together. I might even be able to talk him into going clubbing."

"What a wonderful idea. How thoughtful of you."

"That's me, Mr Thoughtful." He slipped the credit card into his pocket and walked away with a wicked grin on his face. He wasn't being thoughtful, he was being evil. His mother's credit card was going to do a lot more than buy Danny a present. It was also going to help Levi seduce a piece of forbidden candy.

# CHAPTER 16

"What the hell happened to your face?" Levi blurted when Peach opened the door to her apartment. She had on a pair of huge yellow sun glasses but they didn't cover enough of her face to hide the fact she was cut and bruised.

"Keep your voice down." She closed the door behind him and motioned for him to sit down in the lounge.

"Are you going to tell me what happened to your face?"

"If you sit down then I will tell you."

Levi promptly placed his butt down on one of the leather couches. "Now tell me."

He winced in sympathy as Peach removed her sun glasses. The colour of her bruises were fading from purple to yellow and yet she still looked terribly injured, Levi dreaded to think how bad her injuries must have been to begin with.

"Do you want the official story or the true story?" she asked.

"Tell me both." Levi braced himself for the anger he knew that would soon surge through him.

"The official story is that I fell down the stairs."

Levi rolled his eyes. "How original."

"But the true story is Bobby read the nasty review I gave his latest film."

"That fucking prick." Levi shot to his feet. "I'm gonna fucking kill him!"

"Sit down," Peach said sternly. "You will do no such thing."

"He can't hit you and not be dealt to. No. That's not how this fucking works."

"Sit down and stop being my hero, although I do appreciate the sentiment."

Levi shook his head, scowling. "That guy is fucking scum. You wait till I get my hands on him."

"I have already dealt with Bobby so you don't have to worry about that."

Levi was too flustered to listen to her. "Why didn't you tell me about this when it happened?"

"I tried calling you from the hospital but you weren't answering your phone last week."

*Oh God...* Guilt slammed Levi in the gut. "I am so sorry, Peach, had I known I would have answered. You know I would."

"I know, poppet." She flashed him a smile as best she could with her cut lips. "You are the one guy in my life I can always depend on."

"Why didn't you try sending me a text?"

"Because I didn't want this"—she pointed at her busted face—"being stored on anyone's message history. Even yours."

"I would never show anyone."

"I know but I didn't want to risk one of your friends snooping through your phone. I don't want anybody knowing I've been whacked about like a piñata."

Levi didn't laugh despite Peach staring at him like he should find her joke funny. "You have at least told the police, haven't you?"

"Are you mad? I can't press charges. How would that look?"

"What do you mean?"

"I am running one of the country's most read gossip columns. A scandal like this would ruin my reputation. I'm not letting the bitches around town snigger behind my back, because you know that's what they will do. They'll be all smiles and apologies to my face but behind my back they will just say I got what I deserved."

"Not everyone will be like that."

"No, everyone else will be worse."

"How?" Levi frowned.

"Because they will pity me." She stared sternly at Levi. "If there is one thing I fucking hate, it is pity. Now sit back down and let me make you a cappuccino."

Levi heaved an angry breath, fighting against his mind telling him to go jump in his car and drive to Bobby's house. "Fine," he relented and sat down again, furiously tapping his foot.

Peach returned with two frothy cups of cappuccino, gently setting them down on her coffee table.

"I am guessing the review you left was pretty brutal, huh?"

"Brutal is an understatement. I said that the movie was so bad that it made my eyes bleed shit."

Levi sniggered. "That is brilliant."

"I thought so too." She delicately stroked her sore cheek. "It seems Bobby doesn't share our sense of humour though."

"So what is it that you have done to get back at him?" Levi asked, knowing she probably wouldn't tell him. "It better be nasty and painful."

"I can't say, but believe me when I tell you it is brilliant."

"How is it brilliant?"

"I told you I can't say anything." She saw Levi's pleading eyes. "But what I can tell you is that in a few

172

months' time, or maybe a year from now, you will see rumours on the Fitzroy Flyer site and you will be like 'Ohhh, that's what Peach was talking about.' And when you read them you will not say a word to anyone. Promise me?"

"I promise."

"You better, otherwise I will cut your balls off and use them for a purse."

Levi laughed. "I'm rather fond of my balls so I think I will be sure to keep my promise."

"Good boy."

Levi took a sip on his cappuccino, wiping away the frothy moustache it left behind. "I hope the next year goes fast so I can find out what you've done. The suspension is killing me."

"It's killing Bobby too." Peach grinned. "He just doesn't know it yet."

Levi almost wanted to shiver from how cold Peach's voice was. "Whatever it is, he fucking deserves it. And worse."

"You also better promise me that you stay away from him. I don't need you defending my honour."

Levi agreed to her wishes, even if he wanted nothing more than to leave Bobby's face a mushy mess of broken bones. But if Peach said she had dealt with Bobby then she had dealt with Bobby. The pink-haired stunner may have had a petite figure and looked soft and defenceless but Peach was anything but. The girl knew how to take care of people who had wronged her. Levi had wondered if in a past life she had been a hitman.

"Now, poppet. Tell me what is wrong with you?"

"Nothing's wrong with me."

"You may not be the one who looks like a cast member of Once Were Warriors but I know something has been beating you up."

"What makes you think that?"

"Because in all my years of knowing you the only other time I can think of where you have failed to answer my calls was when Sophie dumped you." She then giggled and added, "Not to mention anyone driving the car you pulled up in would be feeling a bit down."

"You saw the bubble on wheels then?"

"I did. It looks like something a real car pooped out its exhaust."

"Tell me about it."

"Why are you driving such a crappy car?"

"Because my stepfather is being a fuckwit and sold the Porsche."

"Why would he sell your Porsche?"

"Because I overspent my allowance this month. He's sold my car and confiscated my credit card. I am officially the most povo Fitzroy Flyer going at the moment. He wants me to get a job and start paying board to live at home. Wanker."

"That's terrible." She looked seriously worried for him.

"He has told me I have two weeks to find a job and start paying him board if I want to stay living there."

"What will you do?"

"I'm not sure," Levi replied, not daring to tell her that he had a blog of his own that could make him money, "I'm just crossing my fingers and toes that something not too soul destroying will come up."

"Interesting." She took another sip on her drink. "What if I told you I know the perfect job for you."

"Working at the paper?"

"No, no. A job for me. It would just be a once off but I would be willing to pay a decent amount."

Levi stretched his arms over his head and grinned. "I always knew this day would come. Do you want me to lick you out here or in the bedroom?"

Peach laughed. "Despite the wonderful things I have heard about your turbo tongue, I was actually thinking of something else."

Levi cocked an eyebrow.

"You study graphic design, right?"

"I do."

"So you would know your way around things like photoshop?"

"Yeah. I'm not too bad." He shrugged. "Actually, I'm pretty damn good at it."

"Perfect. Well, how would you like to be my freelance designer for a top-secret project I am working on?"

"What's the project?"

"You have to promise not to tell anyone?"

"Don't I always promise that?"

"Only Bobby knows this but for the past year I have been writing a book and it's just about finished. I have to send it off to an editor yet to have a final proofread but other than that it's pretty much done. I just need someone, you, to make me a book cover."

"That's awesome. What is it about?"

"It's basically about what it's like to run a gossip-slash-entertainment column and sharing the scandalous secrets I know but with different names and fictional settings."

"I bet it has some juicy stories."

"Oh, it certainly has that."

"Any stories about me?"

"Maybe, maybe not." She simpered. "If I have written any about you then they are only good stories."

"That makes sense since there are only good stories about me to be told."

Peach laughed. "Try telling that to all the girls you fuck and forget."

Levi winked. "You know my motto: love is for the weak."

A brief silence settled between them before Peach said, "You haven't really been scoring many girls lately though, have you?"

"I guess it's been a few weeks."

"Is that why you didn't call me last week? Girl trouble?"

"It was just a busy week," Levi lied.

"You can tell me, poppet." Peach had a glimmer in her eye, the look she always had when she had found out something scandalous.

Levi gave her a droll stare. "What do you know that you're not telling me."

"Don't get mad, it's just a rumour."

"A rumour? What rumour?"

"It's not so much a rumour... it's more just something I got told."

"Isn't that the same thing?" Levi glared at Peach. "Just tell me what it is."

"I had a phone call last week from a certain someone who said they saw you kissing a man's feet."

Levi's heart flipped. "Wh-who said that?"

"Do you really want to know?"

"Of course I want to know whose spreading lies about me."

"Jessica Bridgeman."

*Oh. My. Fuck.* A ghastly heaviness sank down in his stomach, crashing like an anchor to the ocean floor. He didn't need a mirror to know how pale his face must have been.

Peach saw how speechless he was. "Before you say anything, I want you to know that if it is true, I don't care. But I am sure you know that. You also have my word that I won't tell anyone. I know that's rich considering my job but I would never betray you. Never you. Somebody being gay, bisexual, queer is not exactly a big deal these days, however, I also know that in some ways it still is a big deal, which is why I understand if you don't want to say anything... if this got out, true or not, while you wouldn't be ostracised, you would certainly fall down the pecking order amongst the Fitzroy Flyers, which is absolute narrowminded bullshit behaviour but we both know that's what would happen. The world isn't where it should be just yet. Nearly, but not yet."

Levi clasped his hands together and slowly nodded. "What exactly did Jessica say?"

"She rang me asking for advice on what to do with a certain dilemma. I asked her what the dilemma was and she said that she had spent a night at Josh's father's and that her and Josh spent the night in a sleepout while you stayed inside the house. Anyway, she said that in the morning she woke up to go use the shower in the house and as she was passing the kitchen window, she saw you kissing Josh's dad's feet. She insisted that is what she saw and she wanted to know if she should tell Josh or not. She said they weren't officially back together yet, so she was worried how he would react."

"What did you tell her?"

"I told her that she was imagining things and that even if it were true Josh would go down the path of bros before hoes and just say she was lying and maybe never talk to her again."

"Thank you."

"You don't have to thank me, poppet. Just tell me what happened."

Levi ran a hand through his hair, struggling to decide if he should tell his secrets to the one person in town who had the power to totally destroy him with them. *Fuck it*, he decided. He was done with only sharing secrets with strangers online. He craved the warmth that would come from a real friend knowing a bit more about the real him. A friend he wasn't trying to trick into having sex with him. "Do you want the official story or the true story?"

Peach smiled. "Both."

"The official story is that Jessica is a lying bitch who is spreading rumours about me because she secretly wants my dick."

"Most girls in Fitzroy do so I can see how that works."

"And the true story is I did kiss Josh's father's feet. I also let him fuck me. More than once."

"Fill me in, poppet."

"That's what I said to him."

They both laughed, the room filling with a jovialness Levi found utterly relaxing. It relaxed him so much that he began sharing a bag of half-truths with Peach, explaining how Dwight had fucked him twice now—once at Josh's birthday weekend and a second time when Dwight had come to mow the lawns. He didn't say a word about Josh, or Blondie, or the more embarrassing aspects of the sex; like Mark's briefs smothering his face or how he'd called Dwight daddy. That would be going too far, as would be telling her about his blog. Candy Boy was hardcore evidence as to the kind of guy Levi was. A not very nice one. But his words about Dwight and how great the sex was? That was fine, they were just little pockets of exhaled air he was happy to share with her.

"I still don't know why Jessica would ring you for advice? Why wouldn't she come to me and ask me what happened?"

"Because she hates you," Peach said bluntly.

"Jessica doesn't hate me."

"Trust me, poppet. That girl can't stand you."

"How do you know?"

"Aside from the fact I have overheard her say so to others—more than once—I also know she hates you because people *never* ring me with gossip about someone unless they have it in for that person. She wasn't ringing me for advice, she was ringing me to make sure your name was dragged through the mud."

"But she's always so nice to me."

"Most people are nice to people they don't like."

"True that." He scratched his head, puzzled as to why Jessica had it in for him. "I don't know what I did to her to annoy her so much."

"She thinks you're a bad influence on Josh. She is worried that you will lead him astray and open his eyes to the wonders of being a manwhore." Peach rolled her eyes.

"Josh is so not like that though. If he wanted to sleep around he doesn't need lessons from me."

"I know but that won't stop an insecure bitch like Jessica Bridgeman from worrying about a guy like Josh cheating on her, desperate to find any way to curb it from happening. She knows Josh is out of her league and that just makes her more insecure. And now she's got the added worry of thinking you might try kissing Josh's feet too." Peach narrowed her eyes. "Have you... kissed his feet or anything else?"

"No," Levi said vehemently. "Josh is my best mate. That would just be too weird."

"It's not weird. He's hot. Your hot. You should have hot man sex together."

Levi laughed. "You're also hot and we haven't fucked."

"Point taken." A hint of a smile tugged at her mouth. "But don't blame me if I just take a quick moment to fantasise about you and Josh doing the nasty together." She closed her eyes. "I can see it now. Mmm. Such deliciousness."

He waited for Peach to open her eyes and make a joke but she kept her eyes closed, looking like she was hard-out imagining the two together. When it stretched past being awkward, Levi cleared his throat and asked, "I don't want to rain on your man-on-man parade but what should I do about Jessica?"

Peach opened her eyes, giving Levi her full attention. "You need to put her in her place. You can't have her going around telling people what she may or may not have seen. I would have told you much sooner but a certain someone ignored my calls."

"Bad Levi." He slapped himself on the hand. "But how do I put her in her place?"

"I think you have two options. Option one: you make a move on her, she says yes, and you fuck her in degrading fashion. I am talking nasty, animalistic sex that leaves her with sore holes everywhere and leaking more than one fluid if you know what I mean."

"Wow!" Levi wasn't sure if he should laugh or choke on shock. "You are very specific."

"If I was being specific then I would have said you need to fuck her anally and urinate inside her."

Levi got lost to giggles, Peach talking filthy was a smutty treat.

"I'm not trying to be shocking," Peach said blandly. "I am just saying that if you want someone to keep your secret then you need an even bigger secret of theirs, and considering there is next to no dirt on this girl—that I know of—then you need to make some mud to fling at her."

"What is option two?" Levi asked.

"You let me take care of her." The protective instinct in Peach's voice was abundant. She shat on people for a living but when it came to Levi she threw her all into giving a shit about him.

"They are both good options. But which do I choose?" Levi asked, despite already knowing which one Peach would recommend.

"You let me do your dirty work." She smiled. "Or should I say, you let Wade do your dirty work."

"Shit. That is heavy."

"Can you think of a better idea? You know if she becomes the newest Benson Banger then no one will ever listen to a word she says… no one who matters at least."

"But how would you get her to—"

"That doesn't matter. You just leave it with me… if that is what you decide you want to do." Peach stared at him intently, a spooky enthusiasm to her gaze like a witch waiting to cast a spell.

He chewed his lip, debating with himself what to do. There was no fate worse for a Fitzroy Flyer than becoming a Benson Banger. It destroyed your reputation instantly, casting you out to the lonely wilderness of being insignificant. What made his mind up in the end wasn't so much about the damage Jessica could do to his reputation but more the opportunity to score Josh with her out of the picture. "I want you to take care of it."

Peach smiled. "Consider it done."

# CHAPTER 17

"I still can't get over how good you look," Levi said to his stepbrother. "It's amazing."

"You're just saying that," Danny said, a blush pinking his cheeks.

"Nar, buddy. You look fantastic. Seriously."

Levi wasn't entirely lying; Danny did actually look really good. For Danny at least. The geeky boy was wearing slim fitting khaki chinos, a grungy-looking red-and-black shirt which was unbuttoned overtop of a plain white t-shirt, and a new pair of red canvas shoes. He wasn't exactly going to set the fashion world alight with what he had on but the smart casual look Levi had picked out for him flattered Danny in every way possible.

"Thank you," Danny whispered, checking himself out in Josh's bedroom mirror.

It was early Friday evening and the pair were about to settle in for a movie night together at Josh's house. While their own home was large enough that they could usually go unbothered by their parents, Levi wasn't taking any chances. Incestuous things were gonna happen tonight and he needed a place where no one would interrupt those incestuous things from happening. It was imperative it happened tonight, otherwise Levi would have to wait over a week for Danny to get back from his birthday trip down south which he was meant to be departing for in the morning.

Levi had picked his stepbrother up from school earlier that day to surprise him with a birthday shopping spree. Danny had been nervous to see Levi waiting for him at the school gates, having kept a safe distance from Levi since dobbing him in for spending too much money, but Levi acted like everything was fine between them, not bringing it up once. Danny avoided the subject too, never asking how Levi was paying for the multiple birthday treats.

The first place Levi took Danny to was the optometrist and paid for him to get new contact lenses, forcing Danny to put them in and keep them in. The geeky teen had owned contact lenses in the past but never wore them. Today he was going to if he liked it or not. The next present for the birthday boy was a new wardrobe to replace the ghastly shit he normally wore. The final stop, and perhaps the most transforming of all, was a visit to the hair salon where Levi instructed the hairdresser to give Danny a spiky modern undercut.

The changes were all relatively simple but so fucking effective, changing Danny's image entirely. It was like a cliché Hollywood movie where the ugly duckling had transformed into one of the cool kids. He'd gone from looking like a young old person to an attractive teenage guy. Attractive enough that if he could learn not to sound like such a loser then he'd have no worries getting himself a girlfriend.

Watching Danny smiling as he checked himself out in the mirror, Levi felt like it was money well spent. Not because of how good Danny looked, but because of how grateful Danny was for his special day with Levi. He couldn't stop saying thank you and gushing over how "Super" it was to be hanging out with his cool big bro. Danny's naivety and enormous gratitude was acting like lubricant for the inevitable sex he didn't know about.

"Thank you so much for today." Danny smiled at him. "I didn't know I looked like this."

"Believe it because you do look like this." Levi stood behind him, patting Danny's shoulders. "You're a stud, stud."

Danny blushed again. "I don't think I'd go that far."

"Trust me, buddy, the girls at school are definitely gonna notice you when you get back from your trip down south."

Danny's eyes widened. "You think so?"

"Oh yeah. They will notice you alright."

Danny lowered his voice. "Notice me in what way?"

"In the way you want them to… they will be gagging to get a taste of Danny D."

Danny let out a self-conscious laugh.

Some girls probably would be keen to take a ride on him if he turned up to school looking like this. But none of them would have the honour of popping Danny's cheery. That cherry was Levi's to take and it was gonna be popped to smithereens before the night was over.

Danny was a smart boy, the kind of kid who got straight A's in all his classes, but he had the social intelligence of shit-covered gumboot. Danny was so naïve he probably wouldn't even know what flirting looked like, by the time Danny realised he was about to be fucked, Levi's cock would already be half way up his arse.

Levi went and patted the bag of clothes resting on Josh's bed. "Try on the other outfit we bought."

Danny stripped down to his boxers, completely at ease to be half-naked around Levi. It wasn't the first time Levi had seen his stepbrother so undressed but it was the first time he had bothered to take notice. The most noticeable thing about Danny's body was how pale it was, his white skin had a milky-smooth complexion, the kind that would burn easily if he sunbathed. That wasn't much of a surprise to Levi though, he knew his stepbrother was Casper the ghost under his clothes but what was surprising was that the skinny Danny wasn't quite as weedy as Levi had imagined. It turned out Danny was more slim than he was skinny, enough meat on his legs to not be accused of walking around on toothpicks and his torso had a slight hint of definition, including the faintest outline of abs. This wasn't the body of a teenage heartthrob but he was radiating a much more fuckable image than Levi could have imagined.

What Levi found most fascinating about his stepbrother's body was the way it straddled both youth and manhood. Aside from a thin strip of hair below his bellybutton, Danny's torso was boyishly smooth while his legs were covered in a masculine terrain of curly dark hairs just like his father's.

"How come we're having a movie night here and not at home?" Danny asked, slipping on his new jeans. "Won't Josh mind us being here?"

"Josh doesn't care. I am sort of housesitting for him while he's away. And I figured it would be better to have movie night here in case you wanted to have a few drinks and maybe go to town later."

"Drinks?" Danny looked concerned.

"I bought us some Vodka Mudshakes. They are really tasty. I'm sure you will enjoy them."

"But I don't drink alcohol."

"Live a little, buddy. Just try some. I promise you will like the taste."

"But what if I get drunk?"

"One drink won't get you drunk, Danny, and even if it did you are here with me so nothing bad is gonna happen."

"I suppose you're right. One won't hurt." He gave Levi a smile as he chucked on one of his new t-shirts. "I know you won't let anything bad happen to me."

∞

It had been an hour since Danny finished playing dress up in front of Josh's mirror and they were now settled in the lounge talking and drinking. Levi was shocked at how easy it had been to convince the usually scared-of-everything Danny to try drinking alcohol for the first time. He'd expected Mr goody two shoes to fend off the alcohol like it was laced with deadly poison. Not at all. Danny was already on his third drink, happily sipping away and talking non-stop. Levi realised that perhaps what had made Danny such a late starter to drinking wasn't his aversion to it but because he lacked any mates to drink with. Levi had always jokingly asked him if he wanted to go drinking but never seriously, not like tonight where he had a fridge stocked with rows of RTDs.

For the most part the conversation was steady and sprinkled with hearty laughter. They covered a safe and wide range of topics—favourite movies, travel stories, debating the existence of aliens. Nothing too serious.

"Did you want me to grab you another one?" Levi asked, motioning towards Danny's empty bottle.

"Yes, please."

Levi went to the fridge and fetched them each a new drink. When he returned to the lounge, he gave Danny the fresh bottle before settling on the floor in front of Danny's feet.

"Why are you sitting down there?" Danny asked.

"No reason. Just fancied a change of scenery."

A comforting silence fell over the room and Levi sensed that now was the time to steer the evening towards where he wanted it to go. He was hesitant though, not because he felt guilty—Danny deserved punishment for narking on him—but because he wanted Danny to have as much time owning innocence as he could. Such purity was sacred and Danny had more than most young people thanks to his sheltered upbringing. Levi was going to miss seeing Danny's innocent light. But he was also going to enjoy extinguishing it.

Levi broke the silence with a blunt question. "Why do you lie to me about being a virgin?"

"Sorry?" Danny blinked at him.

"Why do you tell me you've had sex before when we both know you haven't?" Levi glared at him.

"I-I don't lie about having sex," Danny stuttered.

"Yes you do." Levi's eyes burned with dominance. He had never challenged Danny all that seriously before about his make-believe sex life but tonight he wasn't backing down.

As expected, Danny crumbled under Levi's dominant gaze. "How can you tell?"

"Because when you've had as much sex as I have, you can spot a virgin a mile away."

"Really?"

"Yeah. It's quite easy actually. That's why those kids at school put your name in that Facebook page. They have probably had sex and can tell that you haven't." Levi knew he was laying it on a bit thick but Danny's naivety didn't allow him to sniff out the bullshit.

"But how can people tell exactly?"

"It's to do with confidence."

"I have"—Danny clasped a hand to his mouth as he hiccupped—"confidence."

"You do," Levi agreed. "But I am talking about *sexual* confidence. There is a big difference." Before Danny could hit him up to explain what he meant, Levi added, "When you finally do the deed, you'll know what I mean."

"Is there a way to make people think you have sexual confidence?"

"By having sex."

"Well, duh. I meant any way to pretend that you have it."

"You can't really fake having sexual confidence." Levi simpered. "It's the kind of thing you can only get from actually getting your dick wet."

"That doesn't solve my problem then."

"Why do you even tell people you've had sex if you haven't?"

"Because I just want people to think I'm less of a dork than what I really am."

"You're not a dork," Levi lied.

"You don't have to be nice, Levi. I know you know how unpopular I am at school. I get picked on for everything. I get bullied for the way I walk, the way I talk, the way I dress. And yep, I get teased all the time about still being a virgin. So I lie and tell them they are wrong, hoping they believe me so there is one less thing I get teased about." Danny was being brutally honest about himself, probably helped along by the alcohol in his veins acting like a truth serum. "And I know I probably shouldn't carry the lies on at home to you but I just want you to think I'm as cool as you are."

This was the part where the caring older brother was supposed to tell Danny that he was as cool as him and that there was nothing wrong with still being a virgin at eighteen. But Levi wasn't being that brother tonight.

"Have you tried asking any girls out?" Levi asked.

"A few times but they either say no or laugh at me." Danny took a swig on his bottle, drowning his glum response.

"Girls can be hard to please," Levi sympathised. "What about guys?"

Danny nearly spat out his drink. "Uh, no! Why would I ask a guy out. I'm not gay."

"I'm not saying ask him out for a date, I'm saying download Grindr and find some horny dude keen to fuck."

"Err. No thanks." Danny pulled a revolted face.

"You don't have to be gay to fool around with another guy, Danny."

"I think it might help."

"Loads of straight guys experiment. They just don't talk about it."

"If it's that common how come you and me haven't done it?"

"You talk for yourself, I never said I haven't." Levi smirked.

Danny gaped. "Really? With who?"

"I don't kiss and tell... or suck dick and tell as the case may be."

"You've sucked a dick before?" Danny's eyes bugged. "Really?"

"I've been known to help a buddy out on the odd occasion." He watched as Danny's innocent eyes filled with questions. Questions that would lead the boy to get so tangled in Levi's web there would be no escape.

"So... you're into guys as well as girls?"

"I wouldn't say I am into guys but occasionally I might see one who I think is hot."

"Do you mean objectively speaking or do they actually turn you on?"

"Sometimes they turn me on but they have to be really hot." Levi took a sip on his drink, flirting with his eyes. "It doesn't happen often but yeah... it does happen."

Danny was oblivious to Levi's sultry stare. "When was the last time a guy turned you on?"

*Bingo! That was the question Levi had wanted.*

"About an hour ago when you were getting changed in Josh's bedroom."

# CHAPTER 18

Danny looked like a stunned meerkat. "Stop being silly."

"I'm not being silly. Seeing you in just your briefs turned me on."

"No it didn't." Danny chuckled. "You said you only like *really hot* guys."

"You are really hot," Levi said, his voice full of conviction. "That's why seeing you like that turned me on."

Danny blushed, his gaze dropping to the bottle in his hand.

"I hope I'm not making you feel uncomfortable," Levi said. "I'm just being honest."

"It's okay." Danny lifted his gaze and smiled. "I just can't believe someone as good-looking as you thinks I am hot."

"Surely you must be able to see how much of a stud you are. If I had my way, you'd sit around in just your underwear for the rest of the night," Levi said, planting another seed of his twisted plan.

Danny coughed out a nervous laugh. "You would actually enjoy that?"

"Fuck yeah." Levi slurped back on his drink, his gaze flicking between Danny's crotch and his face. "You got my wheels spinning earlier."

Danny's blush deepened. "Thanks. I... I'm flattered."

Levi didn't say anything, he just remained on the floor, appearing as casual as possible. It was his job as the predator not to pounce too fast, he needed his prey to come to him.

And then it did.

"Did you want me to?" Danny's eyes darted around the room before returning to Levi. "Sit here in my underwear?"

"That would be seriously awesome if you did but you don't have to."

"You just want to look right? Like no touching?"

"Yeah, man. No touching. I'm happy to just look and admire."

"I don't see the harm in that," Danny said. "It's kind of weird but I'm cool with it."

Stiffly crooked lips and nervously blinking eyes belied the confidence Danny was attempting to exude. Levi knew more than most people the rush that came from feeling sexually desired, and for someone like Daniel Candy who'd never experienced such a thrill the rush must have been enormous. Enormous enough to make the usually sensible teen do something unexpected.

Danny put his drink down and stood up to slowly remove his clothes. First his shoes and socks, then his shirt and finally his pants. He bundled his clothes up and lay them on the couch and sat back down.

Levi sat up straight, hovering forward, smiling with his eyes as they roamed Danny's exposed flesh. He'd been worried he might have to fake his arousal but as his balls tightened in his pants he realised he was more than capable of getting horny from Danny's young body.

"Is this okay?" Danny asked, sat nervously with his knees together.

"Would you be able to spread your legs a bit wider?"

Danny shuffled his feet apart on request, opening his legs up so Levi had an unobstructed view of the sexy bumps in his underpants.

"Oh, man. You are so fucking hot right now."

Danny giggled into one of his hands as he wiped his mouth. "Am I?"

"Fuck yeah." Levi forced himself to laugh self-consciously. "I'm already getting a stiffy."

"Are you really?" Danny's eyes bugged. "You're getting an erection over me?"

"Yep. Can't you tell?" Levi pointed down at his tenting crotch.

Danny gazed down at Levi's crotch. "Wow."

"That's how fucking sexy you are, Danny." Levi rubbed his growing bulge, making sure Danny could see how aroused he was. "You're giving me major wood."

Danny didn't say anything, he just continued blushing and smiling ear to ear. The boy's face was a picture of pride, his ego swelling as much as Levi's dick, but that didn't mean he wasn't nervous from Levi's hungry gaze.

In a bid to tone down his stepbrother's jitters, Levi asked Danny about his plans for university next year, igniting an hour-long conversation about how much Danny was looking forward to life after high school when he would move away to study in Australia. The change of topic worked wonders, slowly peeling the blush off of Danny's face until he was talking like everything was completely normal. It was as if he had forgotten he was half-naked, scratching his nuts more than once quite unashamedly.

When Danny excused himself to use the toilet, Levi decided it was time to up his game and take them to the next stage of the evening. He had to make a move that was more than just visual violation of Danny's young body.

When Danny returned from taking a piss, Levi turned on the flattery again, complimenting Danny on how good his body was.

"Thank you." Danny sat back down on the couch. "I've always thought I'm too skinny though."

"You're not too skinny. You're just right." Levi winked at him.

Danny winked back.

"You wanna be careful about winking back at me, I might get the wrong idea," Levi teased.

"I think it's safe for me to wink back at you. It's not like you actually want to do anything physical with me." He paused. "Right?"

Replying with a vulgar *I am gagging to fuck you up the arse* was not the right move so Levi settled for more PG rated territory. "Then how come I have been sitting here the past hour trying not to ask you for a kiss?"

"You can kiss my hand if you like?" Danny joked.

"I would prefer a kiss on the lips." Levi waggled his eyebrows. "Do you think that would be okay?"

Danny squirmed in his seat.

"Oh, come on. It's just a kiss," Levi said.

"It's not that I don't want to, it's just…" Danny's voice trailed off.

"Just what? Am I too ugly or something?" Levi sniggered.

"Gosh no. Not at all. You know how good-looking I think you are."

"I know girls are more your thing but it's just a kiss, buddy."

"It's not even that," Danny said earnestly.

"Then what's the problem?" Levi scowled, annoyed to be feeling rejected by Danny of all people.

Danny scratched his neck, nerves firing off of him. "I've never kissed anyone before and I don't want to disappoint you."

"You've never kissed anyone? Like ever?"

Danny shook his head. "Never ever."

Levi had never even considered that. He'd always known Danny lied about not being a virgin but he had never stopped to consider the possibility that his stepbrother had never been kissed. "Well, how about I teach you?" Levi stood up, pointing to the patch of floor separating them. "Come on. On your feet. It's time for Kissing 101 with Professor Candy."

Danny laughed. "You're going to give me kissing lessons?"

"You betcha. Now get your arse off the couch and pucker up."

Danny grinned as he wobbled to his feet. The way he swayed gave away just how drunk the few bottles of Vodka Mudshakes had made him. "Is there anything else I have to do other than just pucker up?"

Levi stepped forward, closing the gap between them. "It's simple really. We put our lips together and then I am going to put my tongue in your mouth and you will put your tongue in mine. Yeah?"

Danny nodded.

Levi pressed his lips to Danny's, pushing his tongue forward onto Danny's bottom lip, letting his stepbrother know to open up. Danny did as his lips were told, obediently opening his mouth and allowing Levi in. Levi darted his tongue inside, wrapping it around Danny's, tasting the sweetness of the Vodka Mudshakes. Danny's tongue flicked around like a lizard, short sharp stabs that forced Levi to pull away.

"Okay. That was a good start but this time try and slow your tongue down. Just let it relax against mine, okay?"

They leaned in for another kiss, this time Danny's tongue moved at a softer pace, a little bit too soft, but it was much better than before.

After thirty seconds of locking lips, Levi retrieved his tongue, biting down gently on Danny's bottom lip. "Better. Much better. Now I want you to try and relax your whole body, try falling into the kiss a bit."

"What do you mean?"

"I'll show you."

Levi stuck his tongue in Danny's mouth again, letting his left hand rub Danny's back, dragging his fingers in firm strokes up and down before tickling the hairs on his neck, pressing his body into Danny's. Danny groaned into his mouth, obviously enjoying the touch. Levi returned a groan of his own, rubbing his crotch against Danny's while his hands clawed at Danny's smooth back.

By now it felt like the breathless kissing had evolved from drunken lessons into a very real feverish frenzy. Their lips had become glued together in a full-body kiss, chest to chest, crotch grinding against crotch, cocks perfectly aligned. Their bodies remained pressed together as each other's hands pulled the other in closer, wanting more.

Levi slipped a hand right down to Danny's arse and squeezed, milking another groan from Danny's mouth into his own. Levi then dragged a finger down the line of Danny's brief-covered crack, wishing like crazy he could pull the pesky material out of the way and ram a finger inside him.

Danny's buttocks tensed spasmodically, his straight hole probably quivering in fear from the threat of a dry-fingered invasion.

Levi pulled his mouth free and began planting little kisses up Danny's throat and the side of his neck—nibbling, biting and sucking. He kissed all the way up to his stepbrother's ear which he then licked and nibbled, doing his best to melt down the wall of Danny's sexuality.

Danny's mouth leaked desperate moans and erotic little whimpers, probably unaware as to how damn sexy he sounded. His hands roamed aimlessly up and down the length of Levi's back, no real rhythm or direction to their movement other than to remain anchored close.

"That feels so good," Danny murmured. "Too good."

"There's no such thing as too good," Levi whispered back, licking along the boy's jawline before nipping his way back to Danny's lips and uniting their tongues with another deep kiss. He retrieved his hand from Danny's backside, moving it to the front of the teen's slim body, and dragging his frisky fingers down Danny's barely-there snail trail.

Danny jolted when he felt Levi's hand slip inside the briefs. But he did not pull away.

Levi slipped his hand inside the warm material, crossing the line on his stepbrother's body that went from boy to man. Danny's curly pubes were slightly damp with sweat and very much untamed, Levi doubted if the kid had ever tried shaving down below. He buried his hand deeper, gripping hold of Danny's pecker and discovered that Danny's manhood was hovering somewhere between flaccid and half-erect. The kid might have been straight but his body was reacting positively to the sensual affection Levi was dishing out, his dick flirting with bi-curiosity.

The taboo heat of what Levi was touching—his teenage stepbrother's cock—should've felt awkward, but it was pleasant. So fucking pleasant, in fact, that Levi knew he was no longer doing this solely for revenge, he was going to fuck Danny because he wanted to.

Levi fondled Danny's fuzzy balls, giving them a light tug before grabbing hold of the boy's dick again which began twitching wildly in his grasp and hardening fast. When it became obvious that Danny's dick had swollen to its full size, he tugged the elastic of Danny's briefs down and exposed his cock.

Danny jolted again, this time breaking away from the kiss. He looked down in silent horror as Levi groped his exposed piece.

Levi was relieved to discover his stepbrother's cock was smaller than his own. It was probably just on 5.5 inches with an average girth and curved upwards. The curve was surprisingly flattering and suited Danny's cock.

"Mmm. It's nice," Levi said, giving Danny's dick a good squeeze. "I like how it bends up like that. It's like the curve was made for my hand to hold onto it."

"Oh golly." Danny exhaled shakily. "I can't believe this is happening right now."

"Are you not enjoying yourself?" Levi gave Danny a firm stroke. "It looks like you're enjoying it."

"I don't know what I'm thinking right now." Danny went rigid, watching Levi's hand molest his dick. "This is so weird."

"Just relax," Levi said soothingly, holding Danny's dick tight.

"I don't think this is a good idea, Levi."

"Why not?"

"We're brothers."

"Not by blood."

"It's still doesn't make it—uh, uh, ohhh…" Danny's words got tangled in his throat as Levi gave his teen meat two fast twisting strokes. His knees buckled and he quickly grabbed hold of Levi's shoulders to keep himself from falling. When he regained composure, he lifted his penetrating blue gaze and said very seriously, "What's happening here? This doesn't feel like kissing lessons anymore."

*No shit, Sherlock.*

There was no point in denying where this was heading so Levi just came out with it. "I'm going to fuck you, Danny, and make you a man."

Danny's jaw ticked. "You want to have sex?"

"Let me pop your cherry for you." Levi nuzzled into his neck, giving him more kisses as he kept gripping Danny's cock. "That way no one will ever tease you about being a virgin ever again."

"But that would involve you putting your penis in me," Danny screeched.

Levi chuckled at Danny's childlike horror. "Yes, it would mean I have to put my penis in you."

"I-I don't think I can do that. Sorry, Levi."

"Live a little. You might enjoy it more than you think. And if you're good to me then I'll be good to you." He squeezed Danny's cock while using his other hand to grab Danny's wrist and place the boy's thumb in his mouth, sucking it with a firm tongue to let Danny know exactly what he meant.

Danny's baby blues said no but his dick answered yes with a hot throb between Levi's furled fingers.

"What do you say, buddy?" Levi hitched an eyebrow. "Shall we have some fun?"

Danny's drunken eyes were fuzzy, like there were a million questions swirling around inside his brain. His mouth slowly creaked open. "I'm so confused right now."

The anxiety of Danny's words fuelled a dark fire inside Levi. A fire that burned in every part of his body, but especially in his cock. Rather than try and gently coax the nervy teen towards a taboo fuck, Levi decided he would drag Danny into it. He sank to his knees and pulled Danny's briefs down so they circled the boy's pale feet.

Danny glared down at him in questioning shock. "What are you doing?"

"Showing you how nice I can be." Levi didn't wait for a response, he just stepped off the edge of morality towards another thing he never thought he would do—suck his stepbrother's cock.

# CHAPTER 19

Danny erupted with a low, long groan, the kind a guy made when taking a huge piss. For a split-second, Levi worried that his stepbrother was taking a piss in his mouth, there was that much liquid, but when he tasted the bittersweet taste of precum he calmed down.

It turned out Danny Candy's less than impressive tool was a hardworking manufacturer of teenage ball juice, coating Levi's tongue with an exquisite amount of precum.

"Oh boy. Oh boy. Oh boy," Danny mumbled on repeat while Levi soaked his dick in spit.

Levi clutched Danny's milky-white buttocks, pulling the boy forward, feeding himself more of Danny's virgin cock. He took, and took, and took. Stealing the taste, the manhood, the sexual essence that was Daniel Candy.

Danny's broken record of "Oh boy" slowly ceased and became replaced with deep moans and hitching breaths. His dick kept leaking torrents of precum, forcing Levi to swallow the boy's jizz down his throat.

Levi glanced up and saw Danny looking down at him, his eyes and mouth both open wide while his arms hung limply at his sides. Levi shot the boy a smile through his dick-filled lips and drove his tongue into Danny's piss slit, the source of all that precum.

Danny's eyes shuddered and his body shivered. "Oh fuck."

Levi chuckled, knowing he was doing a good job if

he could make Danny utter a curse word. He dug his tongue in deeper, demanding more of his stepbrother's juice. Danny obliged, his dick leaking larger globs of the bittersweet stuff. Levi swallowed it back and resumed fucking his face with Danny's dick.

Danny's dick tasted different to the Stephenson men; it had a saltier somehow sharper taste. It didn't taste better or worse. Just different. What was also different about sucking Danny was how he was smaller than both Dwight and Josh. Rather than it being a bad thing, Levi actually found he quite liked Danny's lack of size, it meant he could suck deeper and firmer and was able to deepthroat the boy like an experienced cocksucker. He navigated the curve of Danny's dick all the way down to the teen's damp pubes, where the musky tang of ball sweat tickled Levi's nose. The light pong of Danny's crotch didn't turn Levi off at all, it did quite the opposite in fact, zapping his cock with hot pulses as he recalled the stench of Mark's underwear wrapped around his face. Danny's smell was very similar to that of his father but Danny's scent was a weaker strain of the potent stench Mark's sweaty balls produced. The inconvenient comparison was disgusting but it didn't stop Levi's cock straining inside his pants as it triggered the memory of Dwight fucking him brutally.

He shooed the memory away and kept sucking Danny off for another two minutes until his mouth grew tired. He pulled his mouth off Danny's dick and tugged on Danny's hand, lowering the boy to sit and join him on the floor.

Danny's face was flushed, his breath uneven and rough. He gazed at Levi with a wild look in his blue eyes. "That was amazing!" He lunged forward and surprised Levi with a big sloppy kiss to the lips. "Thank you! Thank you! Thank you!"

"I take it you enjoyed that then?" Levi smirked.

"That was more fun than going on a roller-coaster."

Levi laughed. "I can't imagine them having rides like that at Disney Land."

"They should," Danny said. "I'd go on that ride all day."

Levi pulled a condom and lube sachet out of his pocket, placing them on the floor.

"Are those so you can"—Danny's voice lowered—"have sex with me?"

Levi nodded. "Yep. Good sex is safe sex."

"Right," Danny mumbled, resigned to the fact he was about to be fucked in the arse.

Levi stood up and began to get undressed.

"This will count, right?" Danny asked. "I won't be a virgin anymore?"

"It definitely counts." Levi pulled his shirt over his head. "After tonight you won't be on the Verco's Virgin list anymore."

"But how will people know I've done it? I can't say I had sex with my brother."

"You won't say who you had sex with but when you tell people that you've had sex before people will actually believe you because you will have the confidence to back it up."

Danny looked like he was about to challenge Levi's explanation but instead he just nodded.

Levi pulled his pants and underwear down, flicking them away with his foot. He knelt down and wasted no time in rubbering up.

"I can't believe you're gonna put that inside me." Danny stared at Levi's latex-covered cock in wide-eyed wonder. "It's so big. I don't think it will fit."

Levi wasn't used to hearing the word *big* associated with his dick but he could tell by Danny's tone that the boy meant it. "Just lay back and relax, buddy. You'll be fine."

"You'll stop if it hurts too much, right?"

"I'm gonna start slow so just hang in there, it will get easier the longer I'm inside you." Levi gave him a reassuring smile. "You're in safe hands."

"I know I am." Danny smiled. "I trust you."

*You really shouldn't.*

"If you trust me then you won't mind if I take some pictures, yeah?"

"Why do you want pictures?"

"Don't you think it would be cool if we had some photos to remember tonight by. This is a big occasion. You losing your virginity."

"I don't know…"

"What if I show you them later and if you don't like them then I'll delete them."

"Okay," Danny agreed. "What did you want a picture of?"

"You're so damn sexy that I want a picture of everything." Levi stroked Danny's chest. "Now lay down on your back."

Danny did as he was told and Levi got his phone and started taking pictures head to toe of Danny's young body, making sure to capture as much flesh as possible for Candy Boy's followers. When Danny's dick began to soften, Levi gave him another quick suck, resurrecting it back to a full precum-leaking erection so he could capture the boy's bendy dick in its full glory. He then asked Danny to roll over and took another intimate series of pictures of his back half.

"Spread your cheeks for me," Levi asked, stroking Danny's rump.

Danny clutched his buttocks and parted his pale mounds, exposing his dainty little anus. Levi's cock throbbed in response to the purity he was looking at. He didn't have to stick his dick in there to know how tight the boy's arsehole would be. He zoomed his camera in and took five shots of Danny's virgin orifice, wanting a picture to remember how it looked before he fucked and ruined it.

Levi traced the outline of Danny's left foot. "What size shoe do you wear?"

"I'm a size ten," Danny answered. "Why's that?"

"Just curious." Levi patted him on the bum. "You can roll back over now."

Danny rolled over. His glassy eyes focused on Levi's erection, awaiting his sphincter's impending destruction.

Levi gripped Danny's ankles and spread his legs apart, and shuffled in close. He ripped open the lube sachet, slathering it over his cock before rubbing the cool liquid between Danny's cheeks.

"That's cold," Danny giggled, shivering.

Levi didn't say anything, just kept rubbing the wetness around his stepbrother's opening. He regarded Danny's anus for a moment, letting the boy keep his virginity for just a few more seconds. Levi then hooked his hands under Danny's knees, lined his lubed cock up with his arsehole and angled forward, pressing the head of his dick against the entrance of Danny's wet, glistening hole.

"Levi," Danny cried out in a panic.

Levi quickly lowered Danny's legs. "What's wrong?"

"I… I just wanted to tell you I love you."

Levi smiled. "Thanks, buddy. I love you to."

It was a sweet gesture on Danny's part but Levi had little time for sweetness. He pushed Danny's legs back again and slid his cock back to Danny's arsehole and pushed.

Danny grunted as the head of Levi's cock slipped inside.

Levi pushed again, gaining another inch of Danny's virginity. The resistance from the tight muscle was immense, Danny's arsehole desperate to keep Levi out, but he surged forward and sank deeper and deeper into the unexplored territory of Danny's body. Levi felt his cock twitch and swell from the hugging tightness of Danny's hole enveloping the buried part of him. Danny's cute boy face was painted in pain, but he appeared to be resisting the urge to say stop. When Levi pushed again, Danny's arse clamped so hard around him his dick could not move. He held still for a moment, then sank all his weight down and let gravity finish off the job.

"Fuuuck!" Danny cried out, punching the floor with his fists. "Pull it out! Pull it out!"

Levi shut him up with a kiss, sticking his tongue past Danny's lips and wrapping their tongues together. Danny's pained whimpers bled into his mouth but Levi just kept kissing him through the hurt. He held Danny's legs tight, keeping his knees to his chest so he couldn't wriggle away.

Slowly, Danny began kissing him back, his whimpering cries drying up as he gave into Levi's dominance. They laid with their chests glued together, kissing until Danny's whole body stopped struggling and his arsehole accepted the fact it had been taken. Levi pulled his mouth away and straightened up, glancing down at his cock buried balls deep in his stepbrother's arse.

*Fucking hell...*

It was one of the most erotic and sinful things he'd ever seen; Danny's clasping anal lips strangling his cock. He wasn't just staring at sex, he was staring at a moral crime. He'd just slaughtered a boy's innocence, claiming a part of Danny that would forever be his. Danny was too drunk and naive to understand what he'd just foolishly given away but Levi knew. And one day Danny would too.

*I will always be your first.*

He looked back at Danny and smiled. "Guess who's not a virgin anymore?"

Danny winced. "I can tell. I can really, really tell." He reached up and stroked Levi's shoulder. "Can we kiss some more, please? That helps take my mind off the pain."

"Sure." Levi leaned forward and granted Danny his wish, locking lips and kissing the boy like he was a lover and not just a fuck.

With their tongues tied, Levi bucked his hips and started off with a slow-rhythm, his hands holding Danny's hamstrings, keeping his knees against his chest. Each plunge of his cock gradually got longer, deeper, harder, until finally he was fucking Danny's arse at a decent pace. Danny groaned each time Levi's balls thwacked against his arse. He draped his hands over Levi's back, embracing him and the plunges of his dick.

Danny's exhales chased Levi's inhales up a staircase of breaths that grew faster and more desperate. Their chests rose and fell, squelching in sweat pooling between them, Levi covering Danny's mouth with his own. It was spicy, kinky, taboo.

When Levi's lungs burned for air, he unlocked his lips and began kissing Danny's neck instead. He slowed his fucking down to a gentle rocking motion, nibbling and sucking Danny's young flesh, leaving a trail of lovebites up the boy's graceful neck.

Danny seemed oblivious to the erotic markings Levi was giving him, he just kept stroking Levi's back and kissing him on the cheek. "I love you," he whispered in Levi's ear.

Levi ignored the boy's drunken words, concentrating on biting his neck.

"I love you," Danny whispered again.

"Does that mean you also love having my cock in

your arse?" Levi whispered back, taking a page out of Dwight's book on how to fuck and humiliate.

"Yes."

Levi licked his way over to Danny's Adam's apple then rolled his tongue to the boy's chin and bit down with a sexy growl. "Tell me how much you love my *big* cock being in your tight little arse."

"I love it soooo much. It feels like it was always meant to be in there."

Levi smiled wickedly. "Wouldn't that make you a faggot, Danny?"

"I don't know." Danny frowned, genuinely confused. "Does it?"

Levi nodded. "I think it does."

"Am I gay now?" Danny sighed and ran a hand through his hair. "That happened quick."

Levi did his best not to laugh. Danny was much drunker than he'd thought. It was as though being fucked had intensified the alcohol in his veins and made him ultra-stupid. Levi went to say something degrading, another jab to try and humiliate his intoxicated stepbrother. But it didn't feel right. The kid was too drunk to be humiliated and even if he wasn't there was an aura of kindness radiating from Danny and it seemed wrong to mock it.

"You're so fucking adorable when you're pissed," Levi said. He dipped his head below Danny's collarbone and licked down Danny's pale chest, sucking the boy's tiny nipples and flicking them with his tongue. He savoured the boyish smoothness he was exploring, knowing that one day in the future Danny's chest would most likely be covered in a dark mat of hair just like his father. Levi gave Danny's pecs one more swipe with his tongue then lifted his head to gaze into his eyes.

Face to face, gazes locked, they searched one another's soul. There was nothing but awe in Danny's glacial eyes.

Levi smiled and pecked him on the lips. "I guess I better start fucking you harder so you can appreciate this big cock you love so much."

Danny nodded. "Yes, please."

Levi unfurled his body and lifted Danny's legs, resting the boy's ankles over his shoulders. He began thrusting much harder, drilling Danny's tight chute on different angles to chip away the forbidden friction strangling his dick. He loved the view as he fucked him, the slick hairs around Danny's arsehole dragging against his shaft, obscene squelching noises accompanying each plunge of his manhood.

Fuck it felt good to really let loose and unleash weeks of pent-up aggression. Levi knew he was fucking Danny's virgin arse far too hard, risking the boy bleeding, but he couldn't help himself. It had been too long since he'd actually fucked someone and been the one in control. That alone made the sex enjoyable but what made it so much better for Levi was that this was his first time ever fucking another guy. His dick was inside another male's arse and he was humming with alpha pride.

He begun to understand the dark thrill Dwight would have stolen from his body, the boost it would have given the older man's ego to fuck Levi so brutally and emasculate him. Levi hadn't dragged Danny through that level of depravity but this fuck he was busily dishing out was depraved in other ways. *Taboo ways.* Fucking a member of your family was extremely taboo but that wasn't what made skewering Danny's fuck-hole so deliciously illicit. It was because Danny wasn't the kind of kid who was ever supposed to have a dick go up his arse. Danny Candy was a good heterosexual boy from a nice family who was supposed to go away to university, date and fuck two, maybe three, nice girls before getting married and starting a family. That was the path Danny was supposed to be on. Not this—sprawled out naked as his head bobbed around from being buggered so ruthlessly.

Danny squawked and squeaked each time Levi delivered him a long-dicked plunge, and his dick began to shrivel, losing its arousal.

Levi spat into his palm and grabbed hold of the boy's deflating cock and began tossing him off, his fist moving in time with each fuck-punch he gave Danny's battered hole. It didn't take long for Danny to be fully-erect again, leaking ball juice all over Levi's fingers while he let out a series of high-pitched grizzles.

"I think I'm going to…" Danny's words petered out.

"Are you gonna cum?"

Danny nodded breathlessly. "I-I think so."

Levi sped up his wrist action. "Come on then, shoot it for me—show me how much you love this big cock in your arse."

Danny's mouth went wide and his face screwed up as his dick erupted with a cumshot worthy of being in a porno. Then he shot again. And again. And again. Danny's young cock just kept firing out white rope after white rope until his sweat-slick chest was laced with thick semen. More dribbled down his flanks, dripping onto the carpet.

Levi smiled at the abundance of hot spunk Danny had produced. It was nothing short of impressive. He slowed his fucking down and dragged a finger through the boy's hot mess, scooped some up and tasted it. "Someone tastes like sex," he said devilishly.

Danny just lay there breathless, completely fucked out. His body was like a slab of meat, his limbs as limp as his softening prick.

Levi pulled his cock out of Danny's ravaged pit and rolled the condom off. He knee-walked around Danny's tired body then dangled his throbbing erection over Danny's mouth. "Suck it," he commanded.

Danny opened up and gingerly sucked down, his tongue doing bugger all. It was a crap blowjob but that didn't matter, Levi just wanted to see what Danny looked like with a dick in his gob.

Making sure his dick stayed in Danny's mouth, Levi leaned over and grabbed his phone and pressed record on the video camera. He hovered the phone over the huge, sexy mess of semen covering Danny's torso before focusing the phone on Danny's face, recording his dick-filled lips.

"Suck harder," Levi said. "I can't cum unless you suck harder."

Danny obliged, rolling onto his side and ramming more of Levi's meat inside his inexperienced mouth.

"That's better," Levi groaned. "Now play with my balls a bit, pull them gently. Yeah… like that." Levi swallowed, feeling the orgasm brewing in his nuts as Danny jostled his smooth sac in his warm little palm. "I'm gonna cum soon… and you're gonna swallow. I wanna see you swallow, okay?"

Danny hummed back something along the lines of *okay*.

Levi trembled as he got closer to his release. He kept the phone aimed at Danny's face, making sure he captured the moment the boy swallowed a batch of hot cum.

"Oh fuck. Yep. Yep. It's—" Levi grunted and his dick ejaculated inside Danny's mouth, gifting Danny a big sticky mouthful.

Levi's body rolled with shivers as he watched Danny slowly slide his mouth off his cock. The boy looked up and saw Levi waiting for the final order to be followed.

Danny didn't disappoint, smiling at the camera as

he gulped back Levi's swimmers before opening his mouth to prove he'd done as he was told.

"Good work, buddy. That was awesome," Levi said, patting Danny on the hip. He shuffled away and sat on the floor with his back leaning against the couch. He took a sip on his drink he'd abandoned earlier, washing away the taste of Danny's spunk. He waited for his stepbrother to have a post-orgasm meltdown, a straight boy freak-out when he realised what he'd just done.

But Danny didn't have a meltdown. He just calmly shuffled over to the couch and rest his head on Levi's shoulder. "Thank you." He rubbed Levi's arm affectionately. "That was so cool."

"Was it?" Levi frowned. It wasn't supposed to have been "cool."

"I'm so glad you were my first."

"My pleasure," Levi mumbled half-heartedly, taking another sip on his drink.

He didn't want to be touched or bothered now he'd unloaded. The sex was better than he'd expected but that's all it had been. Sex. But that didn't stop Danny sitting beside him like a clingy sidekick, probably thinking they were suddenly besties after such an intimate experience.

Danny stroked Levi's face but Levi ignored him, not in the mood for the teen's drunken silliness. When Danny stroked his face a second time, Levi turned his head and sneered. "Can I help you?"

Instead of saying anything, Danny launched his mouth at Levi's and kissed him on the lips, catching him off-guard.

Levi wasn't sure what to do but he accepted the boy's tongue inside his mouth and kissed him back. The kiss went on longer than Levi felt comfortable with, until finally Danny pulled away and lay his head down on Levi's naked lap like he was about to go to sleep.

"Someone is a very drunk birthday boy, aren't they," Levi said warmly, ruffling Danny's hair.

"That's me, the birthday boy." Danny let out a loud "Whoop!" and waved his hand in the air before it dropped down and rested on Levi's leg.

Levi hoped Danny would now just fall asleep from the combination of booze and empty balls. He suspected that his stepbrother would wake up tomorrow with a nasty hangover and colossal shame from knowing that not only had he given up his virginal arse but he'd also acted like a lovesick girl.

Levi stayed on the floor and guzzled on his drink, stroking Danny's hair while the boy drifted off to sleep. He had been furious with his stepbrother for narking on him but he felt things were even between them now. The pictures and video he had of Danny were going to make one helluva hot story and he knew it would get Candy Boy a tonne of new subscribers.

Just as Levi finished the last mouthful of his drink, the sound of a phone ringing and vibrating sounded behind him on the couch.

Danny shot up right away, apparently not asleep at all. "I better get that. It will be Kaleb. He said he'd ring me tonight." Danny eased himself up from Levi's lap and went and rummaged through his clothes on the couch to answer his phone.

Danny wasn't on the phone long, barely saying much at all, but when he hung up his shoulders were slumped and his face glum.

"What's wrong?" Levi asked.

"Kaleb just told me that he can't go on holiday with me and Dad anymore." Danny settled back down beside Levi and lay his head on his lap again, pulling one of Levi's arms down around him like a blanket.

"What's the dickhead's excuse?" Levi felt annoyed

on Danny's behalf. The poor kid had been looking forward to his birthday holiday for weeks, mostly excited that for the first time he would be having a friend go away on holiday with him.

"He got a tattoo last week and apparently it's got infected."

"He what?" Levi said loudly.

"Kaleb got a tattoo." Danny rolled onto his back, still using Levi's crotch area as a pillow. "It looked poorly done when I saw it so no wonder it has turned bad."

Levi's heart squeezed. "What's the tattoo of?"

"It's really stupid. It's just the letters *DS* in red and yellow ink. He won't even tell me what it stands for." Danny looked up and blew Levi a kiss. "But I guess we all have our secrets."

# EPILOGUE

*Dear Candy Boy*

*I am sorry to hear you are struggling financially. That is never a nice thing. If your next story fails to bring you the income you need then I may be able to help. But you would have to learn to play nice and stop insulting me in your messages. I can be a wonderful friend if you let me, a not so wonderful one if you are rude.*

*Perhaps you could come visit me to discuss an arrangement that could work out great for both of us. You would be able to catch up with Shay while you are here. I am sure he would love to see his little prince. You could both "Hang out" LOL*
*Let me know what you think.*

*Yours sincerely and erotically*

*Demon Dave*

# ABOUT THE AUTHOR

Zane lives along the rugged west coast of New Zealand in a pink shack with his gaming-obsessed flatmate. He is a fan of ghost stories, road trips and nights out that usually lead to his head hanging in a bucket the next morning.

He enjoys creating characters who have flaws, crazy thoughts and a tendency to make bad decisions. His stories are emotionally-charged and don't shy away from some of love and life's darker themes.

Printed in Great Britain
by Amazon

61232592R00132